Zabel Yessayan on the Threshold:

Key Texts on Armenians and Turks as Ottoman Subjects

Translated, Edited and with an Introduction

by

Nanor Kebranian

Gomidas Institute
London

The English translation of this work was accomplished with the support of the Calouste Gulbenkian Foundation. This work appears alongside its Armenian version with the same title, Զապէլ Եսայեան՝ Մեմին Վրայ – Բանալի Գրութիւններ Օսմանահպատակ Հայ եւ Թուրք Կեանք, (Beirut: Pakine, 2023), also supported by the Calouste Gulbenkian Foundation.

ISBN 978-1-909382-75-6
Gomidas Institute
42 Blythe Rd.
London W14 0HA
United Kingdom
www.gomidas.org
info@gomidas.org

CONTENTS

Acknowledgements

I must begin by thanking Peter Magierski, Librarian of the Middle East and Islamic Studies collection at Columbia University, without whose archival assistance this book simply could not have been possible. My great many thanks to Kayane Madzounian at the Calouste Gulbenkian Foundation who assisted in seeing this project through. Thank you, Ara Sarafian, for accepting to publish this book through the Gomidas Institute. And, of course, I cannot thank the Calouste Gulbenkian Foundation enough for funding this work.

Spouses of scholars often do not receive the credit they deserve for the work that ultimately reaches our hands. Words fail in thanking my husband, Rafal, for the teacher, the friend, and everything in between that he has been over the course of these years. And my son, Eliot, for the irrepressible joy and kindness with which he graces our lives.

What Lies Beneath: An Introduction

This book lifts a thick veil of obscurity that has shrouded receptions of Zabel Yessayan's (1878 – 1943?) thought and work for nearly a century. That may seem surprising, given that the past twenty years have witnessed burgeoning interest in Yessayan, notably in Turkey. She has been more widely published, translated, studied, even performed than any other Armenian writer. And, remarkably for a 'minor' figure from a bygone era writing in an endangered language,[1] her notoriety has even penetrated the margins of international literary discourse.[2] Digital and print versions of her biography – including her autobiography – and writings are now freely available in the original Armenian as well as in translations into multiple languages.[3] And there is an abundance of commentary about her life and work.[4]

Much of that discourse has revolved around two nodes of interpretation, one centered on Yessayan as a writer of national catastrophes and the other, on her feminist engagements. The feminist interpretation has spurred much of the recent enthusiasm for Yessayan the woman, especially in Turkey and the United States. She is perceived as a standard bearer of feminism and is frequently upheld as a model of emancipatory thought and action. But it is the psychoanalytic approach to Yessayan as a 'writer of disaster'[5] that has dominated her international literary reception. Her work is now overwhelmingly regarded – and taught – as the expression of traumatic silence and mourning, a chronicle of unspeakable collective violence and irremediable injustice.

While they have broadened Yessayan's readership, both approaches have also led to certain significant misconceptions. The feminist approach has eschewed the complexities in Yessayan's understanding of women's emancipation by failing to engage with her often expressly stated ambivalence toward feminism as an ideology. Precisely the most interesting and often vexing aspects of Yessayan's feminism entail her conceptions of sex, gender, and in/equality. In the same breath as she proclaimed that 'centuries of male tyranny'[6] have created structures of inequality that have stunted women's development, she nonetheless and unproblematically upheld motherhood as the ultimate source of women's 'omnipotence;'[7] that is, without accounting for the ways in which such forms of patriarchally idealized domesticity have intensified women's marginalization. Similarly, Yessayan repeatedly asserted women's inalienable right to work, to exercise their agency in all aspects of their personal and public lives, to be valued as the equals of men. Yet, she also believed in the intrinsic and irreconcilable physical and mental differences between the sexes that make certain fields "unsuited to her [woman's] character and proper for men." "Women and men have equal value, yes," she claimed, "but they are not equal or alike... 'A society can only thrive when it understands what a woman and a man are.'"[18] Yessayan's conceptions of both were fairly conventional. As for feminism *per se*, Yessayan showed great wariness towards its Western modes as they were theorized and practiced in France. Her interactions with bourgeois European feminists quickly enlightened her on the unbreachable gulf separating them from the needs and priorities of poor or working-class women.[9] She was unconvinced by most of the feminist 'activism' she encountered in Europe. And her interactions in such circles led her to the defeatist conclusion that such movements amount to mere pageantry, ultimately incapable of initiating fundamental social change.[10]

Yessayan's feminism was a situated feminism. It was deeply entrenched in local and national concerns. Her advocacy for women's rights, especially the right to work, constituted one thread of her greater concern to bolster the social, economic, and political standing of the struggling Ottoman-Armenian population.[11] Her insistence on the irreplaceable value of women as pedagogues in their capacities as mothers and teachers was tied directly to her broader agenda to fortify Armenian sociality and society through education.[12] Armenian language attainment, retention, and literacy remained a constant challenge especially for Ottoman-Armenians in the provinces, who, as she wrote in 1911, spoke "'the enemy's language'" (original quotes in text).[13] Yessayan's support for the growing number of working Armenian women, notably teachers, constituted a strategic antidote to the threat of cultural and linguistic assimilation.[14]

It is essential to recall that Yessayan's feminist formation took place in the precarious context of Ottoman imperial autocracy and during the rise of the Armenian movements of national liberation. The first 30 years of her life coincided with the despotic rule of Sultan Abdülhamid II (r. 1876 – 1909). When Yessayan's father arranged her 1895 departure to study at the University of Sorbonne in Paris, it was to protect his daughter from this increasingly hostile government. (Yessayan obliquely alludes to this autobiographical detail by projecting it on to the male Turkish character, Feyzi, in this book's final story, "On the Threshold"). Already infamous for its surveillance and censorship system, its brutal suppression of perceived opponents, and its Islamist agenda, by 1895, this government had also demonstrated its willingness to deploy proto-genocidal tactics. The state began to use racist anti-Armenian language[15] and other tactics of 'official othering.'[16] It employed massacres to suppress legitimate opposition to extortionary taxation and other forms of economic dispossession.[17] Forced conversions in the provinces became a method of assimilating and diluting the Armenian presence.[18] Extra-judicial mass incarcerations terrorized the provincial Armenian population through countless instances of heinous – and illegal – torture and abominable prison conditions.[19] And such treatment was reserved mainly for Christian, notably Armenian, inmates who were dubbed revolutionaries and detained as political prisoners. Many of them were children.[20]

None of these crises and atrocities could be aired publicly due to severe censorship. Writing and publishing became volatile and dangerous professions and had to be navigated with tremendous discursive care. Censors and spies were ubiquitous. But working for the state's surveillance system was a precarious enterprise. Many of the censors appointed to Armenian publishing houses or other positions of oversight were Armenian and had to tread a fine line between appeasing the state and protecting their community. Occasionally, they could abuse their position or be coerced to by powerful Armenian figures who would manipulate them so as to discredit and eliminate their opponents. Until 1880, the authority to censor lay in the hands of the censors themselves and could be implemented arbitrarily according to their personal judgment or professional ambitions.[21] Without explicit legal guidelines or pre-publication screening, a writer, publisher, or editor had to use great discretion to avoid investigation and punishment. The musicologist-publisher, Yeghia Dndesian (1834 – 1881), became a notable 'first victim' ('*antranig nahadag*') when he published a songbook that included Mgrdich Beshigtashlian's (1828 – 1868) well-known and widely performed patriotic songs. Dndesian's censor, who was apparently Armenian or somehow knew full well the unofficial lyrics of Beshigtashlian's well-loved 1862 poem/song, "Death of the Armenian Hero" ("*Mah Kachortvuyn*"), reported the musicologist's fatal error.[22] Dndesian was convicted in 1881 and jailed under torturous conditions in an Istanbul (Constantinople) prison. His privations and tortures led to his death a little over two months later.[23] What Dndesian's censor evidently knew was that Beshigtashlian had written the piece as an act of protest against the Ottoman state's repressive measures against the Armenians of Zeytun in 1862.[24] The print version of that poem's closing couplets had always been, "Let the barbarians' mothers weep and you/ Take joyous tidings back to our home." But they were always sung as, "Let Turkish mothers weep and you/ Take joyous tidings back to Zeytun."[25] Writing in 1912, four years after the 1908 Constitutional Revolution that had toppled the previous despotic regime, Teotig (1873 – 1928) wondered, "Nonetheless, in the cemetery of Balıklı, beneath the ancient elms, where is the tomb of this first victim of tyrannical Turkish censorship, who had so passionately served Armenian literature, Armenian music, Armenian printing and Armenian patriotism...? ...And Dndesian's *Songbooks* [*Yerkaran*] had been secretly burned by his relatives as a political strategy of 'thwarting disaster...'"[26] Dndesian's death served as a stark warning to the leaders of Armenian print culture.

Such measures of silencing intensified in the ensuing years. Newspaper editors were arrested, jailed, beaten, and even killed. Journals, where most Armenian literary works were published, could be shuttered indefinitely. Writers had to choose their topics and words exceedingly carefully, and a single misspelling could give rise to investigations and arrests. These circumstances created a pervasive state of suspicion and vulnerability that deeply compromised the already fragile and fragmented class and social relations among members of the Armenian community. Armenian literature published in the Empire could do little to address and redress those circumstances as its forebears from the generation of the 'Awakening' (*Zartonk*) – such as

Beshigtashlian – had previously done, albeit to a limited extent, during the Ottoman reform era (*Tanzimat*).

But it would be a mistake to conclude that Ottoman-Armenian print culture was reduced to total silence on the conditions and consequences of despotic rule, and that the Armenian public had no outlet for its grievances. Clandestine publications that were printed abroad were smuggled and circulated among Ottoman-Armenian readers. Armenian political parties, publishers, and educational and religious institutions in major European centers such as Vienna, Venice, Geneva, Paris, and London produced an abundance of literary, polemical, journalistic, and scholarly material addressing numerous aspects of the Armenian national plight. Ottoman-Armenian activists and intellectuals who had taken refuge in Europe – including Yessayan – began to forge a language for articulating experiences of domination that would become the bedrock for its further elaborations following the Second Constitutional Revolution (also known as the 'Young Turk Revolution') of 1908. Émigré Armenian literature of this era is replete with narratives of resistance – much of it influenced and colored by the language of the Armenian nationalist-revolutionary movements, but much else that exceeded their ideological limits and innovated uniquely subversive expressions.

Yessayan was an exemplary craftswoman of such narratives. Many of her stories written between 1895 and 1908 illustrate her extraordinary acuity as a writer of anti-imperial resistance. Those works enabled her to develop the linguistic techniques and thematic strategies on which she continued to draw at times of political and discursive precarity for Ottoman-Armenians. She devised apophatic methods of saying and unsaying, revealing by concealing, ventriloquizing by deflecting, empathizing by antagonizing and *vice versa* using a host of techniques. These included but were certainly not limited to metaphorical layering, symbolic substitutions, suggestively familiar but displaced terminology, telling elisions, persistent recurrences, autobiographical references, intertextuality, and much else. There is no way to do justice to quite all that Yessayan developed into her anti-imperial literary arsenal in this brief introduction. But this compilation provides a set of underread, misread, or previously unknown works that enable readers to witness and appreciate Yessayan's dissident craft directly. These include my recent discovery of three 1914 essays and fiction ("On the Question of Turkish Women's Emancipation;" "The *Namehram*: Life as a Turkish Woman;" and "The Wait") addressing the rights of Turkish women.[27] Hitherto unknown and uncatalogued, they are documented and presented here for the very first time.

Covering a span of 25 years, the works in this volume demonstrate Yessayan's lifelong preoccupation with conceptualizing and representing the crises of Ottoman subjecthood. She pioneered a literature that explored – to borrow from Judith Butler's influential title[28] – "the psychic life of power" in the Ottoman Empire or the psychic life of Ottoman power. This experience constitutes almost uncharted terrain in scholarship as well as in public discourse, an alarming lacuna especially in the study of Armenian history and literature. My article on the life and work of Hagop Oshagan (1883 – 1948) – "Lost in Conversion: Mourning the Armenian Turk" (2012)[29] – initiated a first step in filling that gap with an attempt to address the topic equitably.

Some decades ago, Gisèle Littman, better known as Bat Ye'or, tried to historicize the experience of Ottoman subjecthood less equitably through her conception of '*dhimmitude*,' – a term that was once used by the sectarian Christian President of Lebanon, Bashir Gemayel (1947 – 1982). Ye'or popularized the term in academic discourse. Referring to the legal designation of non-Muslims – *dhimmi* – she argued that their status as political and social unequals under Islamic rule drove them to a "state of fear and insecurity" and a forced acceptance of "a condition of humiliation and of total inferiority to Muslims."[30] Recent Ottoman-Armenian historiography has uncritically employed Littman's term. One historian of post-genocide Istanbul has suggested that there is a continuity between Ottoman-Armenians' experience of so-called *dhimmitude* under imperial rule and the 'secular *dhimmitude*' or 'neo-*dhimmitude*' of the Armenian minority in Republican Turkey.[31] It would be mistaken to accept that approach or to employ Littman's problematic term *dhimmitude*. The reason is that Littman's work has a notorious far-right Islamophobic agenda. She helped propagate the so-called 'Eurabia' conspiracy theory, which claims that the EU is selling

Europe to the Islamic world in exchange for oil. And she has conferred and publicly allied with militant rightwing ultranationalists.[32]

It behooves scholars – *especially historians* – investigating the Armenian social, cultural, and psychological dimensions of subjecthood to plumb the Armenian sources – including invaluable literary texts – for indigenous terminology and conceptualizations of those experiences. That is no easy task, considering the volume of available material; the dearth of reliable scholarship addressing the topic; or, worse still, the availability of misleading, historically inaccurate, or de-historicized literary studies.[33] Moreover, it requires Armenian language proficiency and a commitment to rigorous archival research.[34] But, while difficult, that task is necessary and certainly not impossible. The indigenous language of Ottoman-Armenian subjecthood has its own terminology, its own conceptualizations, as evidenced by hitherto unacknowledged sources attesting to that experience. For instance, Armenian revolutionary periodicals addressed it as '*sdrgutyun*' (slavery); Armenian writers such as Oshagan referred to it as '*gerutyun*' (captivity); while others qualified it in terms of '*paroyagan rayayutyun*' (moral rayahood). With various emphases, these commentators grappled with the experience of Ottoman-Armenian subjectivity as an agglomeration of alienation, moral degradation, and terror issuing from a hierarchically delineated ethno-confessional context where Muslims ruled over non-Muslims.

Many of Yessayan's pieces in this volume depict those named states of subjecthood through images and descriptions of captivity. Cages, window bars, unbearable physical burdens recur as central motifs, often to evoke a spirit of solidarity with 'foreign' enslaved, captive, and subjugated others. Yessayan's emphasis on the black eunuch's painful racialization in "The *Yashmak*," for example, reflects her understanding of the untold atrocities issuing from European colonial slavery. Having lived in France and imbibed its culture and history, she would not have been ignorant of the country's brutal history of enslavement, especially in Haiti. And her sympathetic portrayal of the eunuch's blackness as a mark of his paradoxically enforced invisibility/subordination in the institutionally differentiated Ottoman context draws a direct parallel with the racially othered European colonial experience. The black eunuch, the non-Muslim Ottoman subject, and the Ottoman Muslim woman overlap and join in her story as various facets of imperial domination.

Since Edward Saïd's publications of *Orientalism* and *Culture and Imperialism*, it has become almost taboo in US leftist postcolonial academic circles to suggest that non-Europeans – let alone Islamic empires – also exercised destructive forms of imperial domination. This hegemony of the margins has created a risk of being called 'Islamophobic' whenever attempting to address entirely legitimate and well-grounded critical approaches to the repressive facets of Islamic autocracy.[35] Saïd himself noted in *Culture and Imperialism* that simply because he does not discuss the structures of domination in the Ottoman Empire does not mean that "Istanbul's rule" has "been either benign (and hence approved of) or any less imperialist [than European imperialism]."[36] He was referring to Istanbul's rule in the Arab world.

Long before Saïd raised the question, Yessayan was grappling with the impact of Ottoman imperialism in (what was once) the Armenian world. This collection of stories and essays provides the first clear illustration of Yessayan's sustained engagement with the nature of Ottoman subjecthood as it affected both non-Muslims and Muslims. These writings are by no means Yessayan's only accounts of that experience. Another volume's worth exists – including previously unknown and uncatalogued published texts – that will become the body of a forthcoming collection. Unlike those texts, however, the eleven pieces in this book constitute a remarkable but previously unremarked thematic intervention: with the exception of the enigmatic story, "His Hate," they all tackle the issue with reference to the experiences of Turkish women.

In that respect, they reveal a technique that Yessayan had first encountered and subsequently adopted in the poetry of Bedros Tourian (1851 - 1872), her great hero as evinced in one of the final chapters ("Bedros Tourian's Grave") of her memoir, *The Gardens of Silihdar*. That technique consists of an ethno-religio-gendered metaphor in which the representation of Muslim/Turkish women as marginalized, silenced, and subjugated Ottoman constituents serves to depict the status of Armenians and non-Muslims more broadly. Tourian's 1871 poem,

"The Turkish Woman" ("*Trkuhin*"), initiated that metaphor, although it has been read at face value as a risky Orientalist foray into Armeno-Turkish desire – an underreading or misreading that has persisted for generations. Yet, like Beshigtashlian's poems and songs from the same tumultuous years of Armenian suppressions in the interior provinces and the formalization of Ottoman censorship, Tourian's contemporaries would have recognized this piece as an optical illusion, the display of something more than meets the eye. The title itself functioned as a kind of veil, a red herring meant to mislead censuring eyes from the fact that the poem also served as a veiled expression of Ottoman-Armenian subjecthood. Lift that veil, look beyond it, and the precarious condition of Ottoman-Armenian existence becomes wholly and instantly recognizable: The "Turkish woman" is a confined, concealed figure entombed and isolated by circumstances that are beyond her control; discernible through a (twilit) "horizon in flames;" poised, despite her youth, beauty, and potential on the threshold of existence, being and non-being, as Oshagan would later put it; her gaze (thus knowledge) and speech restricted; and her immense passions suppressed, "still deprived of a horizon" to call their own – like the Armenians depicted in Tourian's overtly patriotic 1868 piece, "The Armenian's Anguish" ("*Vishdk Hayun*").[37] Moreover, Tourian the consumptive Armenian poet figures this ostensible Turkish woman empathetically in his own image as a waxen, pallid creature perched on the verge of death. The similitude characterized through his loving words thus bear forth the synthesized figure of an 'Armenian-Turk.' "Even if she dies/," he writes, "You'd say – she is now born (Թէ իսկ մեռնի՛,/ Կ՚ըսես — հի՛մա կը ծնի).[38] Ultimately, "The Turkish Woman" presents a frustrated yearning for freedom – the freedom to live and to commune unconditionally that characterized much of Ottoman-Armenian life. But Tourian knew to employ seemingly innocuous naturalistic imagery to delimit this drive for emancipation, and therefore, to forestall suspicions of fomenting dissident Armenian sentiments. The Turkish woman is a butterfly one moment, a bee the next. What could be more innocent? And what could be more ingenious…

Yessayan's first piece in this collection, "The *Yashmak*" (1899) – a type of veil –, even supersedes Tourian's innovation. Where generations of post-genocide Armenian readers have failed to recognize Tourian's ingenuity, Yessayan clearly understood his technique and borrowed it. She was a formidable reader – perhaps a better reader than a writer in some ways. And with "The *Yashmak*," she took up the mantle of her beloved forebear by conceiving a story that circumvented the almost inescapable snare of Abdülhamid II's censors; a story in which a Muslim woman stands in as an ethno-religio-gendered metaphor for the status of subjugated Ottoman subjects – notably, Armenians. Yessayan even makes an imagistic nod to Tourian by similarly likening her story's heroine to a butterfly. And she further amplifies such naturalistic imagery by rendering an additional likeness to a caged bird attempting a f(l)ight for her freedom. But Yessayan does not stop there. She digs even deeper to suggest an even darker, more authentic metaphor in the figure of the black eunuch. Ottoman-Muslim women, her story suggests, may be subjugated and confined, but they can nonetheless be beneficiaries of the Empire's confessionally communalist system. They can enjoy the associations, affections, gifts, and protections of their co-religionist rulers, however capricious they may ultimately be. Those outside that fold, however, could not hope even for such capriciously bestowed privileges. Yet, ultimately, this difference is negligible. The constraints of ethno-confessionally defined patriarchal hierarchy – captured in the metaphor of the *yashmak* – lead to the same "bonds of fate," as the story concludes. According to Yessayan, those bonds do not culminate in commiseration or solidarity. Their most pernicious effect is precisely to prevent recognition and bonding, to disable the conditions of sociality, as the eunuch's and his mistress's mutual states of persistent isolation reveal.

"The *Yashmak*" is the key to unlocking the layers of meaning in the stories that follow, including "His Hate." It alerts readers to the encoded nature of Yessayan's – and her contemporaries' – literature. "His Hate" constitutes a cipher for the paradoxical dynamics of domination/subjugation, where truth and lie, innocence and guilt, terror and infatuation, pain and pleasure undergo perversions of meaning. Victimizers present themselves as victims, while the victims search for their own guilt in the perpetrator's crimes. As a meditation on the apparently inexplicable source of 'His' hate, the story nonetheless provides clues suggesting that it arises from exploitations of perceived differences in an uneven power structure – 'He' is taller and stronger; she, small and inconspicuous. To that end, the 'antagonists' are, among other contrasts, conspicuously color-coded – dark- *vs.* light-complexioned, black *vs.* blue eyes, bright *vs.* shadowy expressions. Still, it would be facile to assume a direct equivalence between darkness and Empire. Yessayan's piece is too intelligent and too subversive for that. And its various paradoxes might suggest the contrary. However, the cadaverous perpetrator's vampirical traits do correspond directly with Yessayan's comparable iteration of the (V)Empire in this collection's final story, "On the Threshold" (1924). Being fluent in French, Yessayan would have noted the perfect consonance in the French pronunciations of '*empire*' and '*vampire*'. Tellingly, she settled on that predatory imagery years after crossing numerous treacherous thresholds herself, both literally and figuratively, from state borders to ideologies.

The first of these was her 'return' from Paris to Istanbul in 1908 on the eve of the Young Turk Revolution, which promised to reinstate the Ottoman constitution, restore parliamentary rule, and deliver free and fair governance to all. Hundreds of Armenians who had taken refuge abroad during the reign of Abdülhamid II returned with high hopes of finally becoming equal citizens in the same country. But those hopes came crashing down just months later, when a 'counterrevolution' paved the way for new and unexpected collective violence by Muslims against Armenians and other Christians in Cilicia. Known as the 1909 'Adana Massacres,' these atrocities resulted in tens of thousands of deaths and untold devastation perpetrated over just a few weeks. The new government's reluctance and/or failure to appropriately prevent, quell, or punish the atrocities sent a clear – and familiar – signal to Armenians. Yessayan read them all too clearly and up close. In 1909 and at the behest of the Armenian Patriarchate, she joined a humanitarian delegation to oversee the collection and placement of thousands of surviving Armenian orphans. Yessayan's trip lasted three months, but she returned to Istanbul without completing her mission. In the meantime, however, she had visited numerous sites of massacre and ruin, spoken with victims and witnesses, and amassed a devastating volume of information about the motivations, methods, and aftermaths of the events. She compiled her findings into the now renowned 1911 chronicle, *In the Ruins.*

This book's overwhelming reception over the past two decades has precipitated contradictory outcomes. On the one hand, it launched Yessayan and this event into a broader public consciousness that, notably, breached the Armenian-Turkish divide; and, on the other, it eclipsed the vast corpus of Yessayan's other works. Importantly, these include her fictional stories based on the same events and published the same year as *In the Ruins* in various periodicals.[39] Presented in this volume as an important complement to Yessayan's chronicle, "The Curse," "Safiyeh," and "The New Bride" (1911) may disrupt readers' assumptions about the writer's literary and psychological responses to these events.

For the past twenty years and based on narrow or presumptuous readings of *In the Ruins*, Yessayan's interpreters have presented a writer and a work that exemplify traumatic silences; "muffled astonishment;"[40] evasion and disavowal. With the exception of Krikor Beledian's foundational reading,[41] much of these conclusions have stemmed from an overemphasis on the work's Preface (as presented by Marc Nichanian) and with an overreliance on the convenient findings of Trauma Studies. Yessayan's chronicle is unquestionably a "testimony" or a representation of many traumas, collective and individual, physical and psychological, social and political, past and present. But certain claims about Yessayan's motivations and purpose simply do not align with the tone and content of the work or with Yessayan's stated aims. The assertion that she, "a modern Antigone,"[42] wrote "not for moral or political reasons, but because she knows she is threatened...by madness"[43] does not correspond with Yessayan's own prefaced statements that the purpose of this work is to oppose authoritarian elements in the country's leadership and to salvage the reputation of the maligned – or defamed – innocent victims, "so that no one would dare approach those wretched creatures with contempt and hatred."[44] Yessayan's work is self-avowedly moral and political in numerous ways, but especially insofar as she recognized from past Turkish political machinations that the victims would be doubly victimized by official denialism, which she strove to counter with *In the Ruins.* That is why she insists emphatically in her Preface that those "wretched creatures" were the ones who at any cost were willing to rise up against "the greatest threat to the country, against the return of tyranny, in whatever new form or guise it appeared. *Wasn't that already the main crime that was imputed to us and isn't that what was invoked as being our racial [tseghayin] ambition?*"[45] (emphasis added).

What Yessayan is referring to here is the slander and scapegoating of Ottoman-Armenians during both the previous despotic regime and the contemporaneous constitutional one as a *race* of insurgents. This denunciation is what had underwritten prior atrocities against Armenians – certainly those perpetrated during Abdülhamid II's rule, but also earlier. Such defamations over the course of decades had established the discourse of an Armenian threat of which Yessayan, her contemporaries, and her antecedents were all too aware and sought actively to combat and overturn. And what they were all witnessing with the government response to the Adana Massacres was a repetition of the same political strategy of defamation *cum* denialism being exercised by the new regime. They knew too well how these strategies were employed both in advance of planned atrocities to rationalize them and *ex post facto* to justify them. The government's demonstrable willingness to employ or permit the use of the same tactic signaled to Yessayan and her peers the ominous portent of more bloodshed.

That is why *she precisely does not interpret the Adana Massacres as a necessary sacrifice* - that is, *not after* her humanitarian trip to Cilicia. Nichanian misrepresents or misreads a prefatory statement by Yessayan to claim that she believed "[t]hese bloodied existences were sacrificed to 'the fatherland.'"[46] What Yessayan states is that after the suppression of the counterrevolutionary uprising in March 1909, when both Armenians and Turks defended and died for the new constitutional government, news of the Adana Massacres were received by her and her compatriots as a painful fact, which they rationalized – "to pacify our anguish" – "by clinging to this idea: 'We too have contributed our victims, this time our blood flowed alongside that of our Turkish compatriots; this shall be the last time."[47] That is how "our eyes knew to continue smiling and…our hearts beat the strongest" during the "extreme joy" felt for the constitutional victory, claimed Yessayan.[48] But everything changed when she left for Cilicia, and the rationale of mutual sacrifice collapsed. Yessayan could not be clearer: "It was in the midst of all this that I had to leave for Adana to aid in caring for the orphans. It was in the midst of this that our *faith shaken, our hearts shattered, our hopes ruined*, we had before us a bloodied, incinerated province... and *there were no moral expectations* [եւ ոչ մէկ բարոյական ակնկալութիւն]..."[49] (emphases added). These are not the words of a woman who clung on to the idea that the Adana Massacres were a sacrificial bloodletting which would still ensure the possibility of peaceful coexistence, as Nichanian avers. He states, "Zabel Essayan...does all that she possibly can to explain that she is not writing in order to speak of affliction and vengeance or from a sense of belonging to a people, to a faction in a multiethnic state. She proceeds as if ethnicity were henceforth a private affair somewhat like religion in the modern state."[50] This mystifying conclusion fails to correspond with Yessayan's bold statements suggesting the contrary: namely that she and her peers lost faith, lost heart, lost hope, and lost trust – both moral and judicial – in both the prospects of peaceful coexistence and the government that feigned to deliver it. That hopelessness is evident in Yessayan's pervasive use of the word "race" (*tsegh*) as opposed to "nation" (*azk*) or "people" (*zhoghovurt*) to refer to the victims and Armenians more broadly. In one instance, she describes the "Aryan" (*Ariagan*) eyes of an Armenian bystander.[51] Thus contrary to Nichanian's claims, not only does Yessayan not treat ethnicity as a private affair, but her language in fact illustrates her belief following these events that Armenians are and will continue to be perceived and treated as an alien race on their own native soil.

With that realization, *In the Ruins* becomes as much a search for a way out of the wreckage as a testimony to it. And Yessayan seems to arrive at two possibilities. The first is Armeno-Turkish solidarity as stipulated in her preface in which she explicitly states her intentions to elicit the empathy, understanding, and trust of her liberal non-Armenian 'compatriots.' She seems to hope that such solidarity will facilitate and support armed Armenian self-defense so that just as Armenians "contributed their victims" for the constitutional fatherland, so will their Turkish counterparts. To that end, the book strategically includes several stories of heroic Turkish defenses of Armenians. More importantly and under the given volatile circumstances, Yessayan unequivocally believes in the significance of organized militant self-defense of the Armenian population to forestall further collective violence. But she is careful to present that belief obliquely by retelling cases of successful armed resistance even against the odds and by subtly indicating where such resistance would have spared lives and properties had the appropriate measures been in place. Most of all, Yessayan does not exculpate the current government or treat the crime, as Nichanian has it, as the expression of the prior regime's final thrashes in its dying days. No modern Antigone here; but possibly, a modern Cassandra speaking unheeded prophesies.

The uncannily prophetic stories, "The Curse," "Safiyeh," and "The New Bride" constitute an expository complement to *In the Ruins* that has remained, until the advent of this book, entirely unheeded. Yessayan composed these fictionalized accounts of Turkish perpetration told from a Turkish perspective as parallel texts to be read alongside her chronicle. The rage, hate, love, empathy, revenge, lament, and regret that she refused to fully articulate in her non-fiction, she gave an almost deafening voice to in these stories. Ironically, they have fallen on deaf or stopped-up ears. But, *In the Ruins* can only impart its full truth when we immerse ourselves in the fiction of these overlooked texts. Yessayan established an undeniable intertextual connection. No one had noticed until the present book's conception that the eponymous character of "Safiyeh" and the bloodthirsty killer of "The Curse," Habib, share their names with the Safiyeh and Habib of the chronicle's chapter, "A Day of Relief." (Yet another Safiyeh appears in "On the Threshold"). Of course, the chronicle and the stories, the fact and the fiction were intended to be read side by side, because the truths that were concealed in each genre were bared in the other. This was Yessayan's most elaborate anti-denialist achievement yet, both for her time and, presciently, for ours. But her voice was lost in history.

In 2015, a Turkish historian, Cengiz Aktar, seemed to hear it or some version of it as he took stock of his country's degraded state. Writing on the eve of the genocide's centenary – when so many seemed to be jostling perversely for their moment in the limelight –, his piece,

"Entering 2015," meditated somewhat naively on the idea that the "the evil haunting us...and our inability to recover from afflictions may be due to a century-old curse and a century-old lie." In a peculiarly superstitious manner that chimes almost word for word with the desperate laments of Yessayan's stricken Turkish characters in "The Curse," Aktar continued:

> This is perhaps the malediction uttered by Armenians, children, civilian women and men alike who died moaning, and buried without a coffin... Perhaps, the massacres which have not been accounted for since 1915 and the charge [sic.] which have remained unpaid are now being paid back in different venues by the grandchildren. The curses uttered in return for the lives taken, the lives stolen, the homes plundered, the churches destroyed, the schools confiscated, and the property extorted... 'May God make you pay for it for all your offspring to come'... Are we paying back the price of all the injustice done so far?... It seems as if our society has been decaying for a century, with festering all around... The denialist prose that consists of three wizened arguments that consist of upheaval, collaboration with the enemy and victimisation —it is rather Armenians who killed us— will continue to be parroted in a series of conferences. And we will dance to our own tunes... The Armenian Genocide is the great catastrophe of Anatolia, and the mother of all taboos in this land. Its curse will continue to haunt us as long as we fail to talk about, recognise, understand and reckon with it.[52]

The spirit of Yessayan's three 'Adana stories' certainly anticipated this superstitious response *before* 1915. Ever the consummately incisive reader, she was able to predict with perfect accuracy the inevitable economic, social, and psychological degradation that would afflict the society of perpetrators; as well as the fact that they would interpret these 'evils' as their victims' curse rather than the logically inexorable consequences of a hierarchically differentiated society. Yessayan's stories do not cast a curse or lend credence to such superstition; rather, they ridicule it. They show up this superstition as the continued self-disavowal, the persistent denial in the very pits of an Ottoman/Turkish society that seeks the explanation for its miseries and their remedies in extrinsic conditions. Aktar suggests that contemporary Turkish society's inability to confront the difficult questions of its past constitute the aftermath of 1915, "a loss [*sic.* of] wisdom deriving from the Genocide." Yessayan's accounts present that loss rather as what I term a *foremath* – the always already inevitably and undeniably genocidal nature of an Ottoman/Turkish society founded upon policies and practices of domination through differentiation. Genocide was encoded in the very foundations of the Ottoman system. Its manifestation was only a matter of time; its enactment a near certain probability. The future of genocide and its aftermath reflected the foremath of its antecedent violence – not just the massacres, of course, but the confessionally communalist society itself. It was not difficult for Yessayan – and some of her other contemporaries – to perceive that a society that remains incorrigibly differentiated could only head in one direction: self-destruction. Premised on policies of scapegoating, othering, and disavowing, it will fail to recognize its faults and deficiencies, only to awaken painfully one day to a world collapsing on itself.

A true constitutionalist patriot, Yessayan was desperate to forestall such an eventuality as a matter of personal, cultural, and social survival. And she appealed to the only Ottoman Muslim constituent that she deemed capable of grasping the situation of subjugated non-Muslims: Turkish women. Her 'Adana stories' voice that appeal through explicit references to Turkish women's suffering and contrition, their repugnance with their men's violence, their fear for their children's lives, and their affection for their Armenian sisters. Few Turkish women would have been able to read these stories, and perhaps Yessayan hoped that they would be translated into either French or Ottoman Turkish. According to Léon Kétchéyan's findings from Yessayan's correspondences, she did in fact have several of her Armenian language pieces translated into Ottoman Turkish and published in Istanbul, and she was already well-regarded in Ottoman-Turkish circles in 1908.[53] Irrespective, she may have legitimately hoped that her intervention even within the limited audience of Armenian readers would mobilize a discursive momentum that would ripple beyond her language community's sphere and into the circumscribed domain of Muslim women.

Over the next four years, Yessayan intensified that momentum through her continued representations of Turkish women in both fiction and non-fiction. With often overlapping themes and spanning the period just prior to the First World War, through the genocide, and then the exclusionary 1923 founding of today's Türkiye, these pieces advocated pacifism; argued for the rights of Muslim women; presented the gendered miseries of persecuted and displaced Muslims; and depicted the patriarchal perils of ethno-nationalism especially for Muslim/Turkish women. "The Glory" (1913), "The Wait" (1914), "The Veil" (1914), "The Death of a Child" (1919), "On the Threshold" (1924), and "Meliha Nuri Hanum" (1928) thread these themes to illustrate the frequent double-binds that perpetuate Turkish women's subjugated juridico-political status in the Ottoman Islamic realm. And to varying degrees – and perhaps least of all in "The Wait" –, each story constitutes an offshoot of Yessayan's borrowed technique in "The *Yashmak*," where the representation of Turkish women veils a deeper commentary on the concomitant struggles of non-Muslim/Armenian subjects. For the discerning reader, the two become almost indistinguishable – or, perhaps more accurately, like a *yashmak*, they serve as the conspicuous sign of the other's absented presence.

Even Yessayan's essays on the question of Turkish women's rights employ this layered characterization. In discussing the legal and psychological dimensions of Turkish women's repression, the two essays – "On the Question of Turkish Women's Emancipation" and "The *Namehram*: Life as a Turkish Woman" – find subtle ways to articulate the comparable experiences of other oppressed and marginalized constituents; and, importantly, the dangers of tyranny. By 1914 – when Yessayan penned these essays –, the Ottoman government led by the Committee of Union and Progress (CUP) had assumed a recognizably authoritarian form. Many who had trusted in their mutually shared revolutionary ideals of constitutional, representative, egalitarian government no longer believed that they would be achieved. These included not just marginalized ethno-confessional communities, but also, as Yessayan reminds her readers, Muslim women. Her essays alert readers that a government premised on differentiated and subjugated constituents only amounts to tyranny. And that tyranny will always stunt progress and provoke distrust, ultimately leading to internecine conflict. And so, her stark warning: "When tyranny is so unjust and so absolute that the oppressed are compelled to feel justified when they indiscriminately exploit the very first available opportunity to help themselves, then all moral foundations can be deemed compromised; and so, even if not everything may be forgiven, everything nevertheless becomes possible."[54] At a time of increasing tension, dread, and hopelessness, this statement strives to alert the governing elites that continued repression will inevitably lead to social instability and civil unrest. It also warns the state that such measures will ultimately compel victims to seek salvation from their adversaries.

Many of Yessayan's observations are sadly as pertinent and true today as they were over a century ago. While the women of Iran risk life and limb to remove the veils obstructing their dignity and freedom; while the women of Turkey struggle to preserve and reclaim the hard-earned rights being overturned by their government; while the women of Armenia live in fear of the men in their own homes, this collection of Yessayan's writings provides a reminder that solidarity for the attainment of greater ideals is always possible even across the most contested battle lines

ENDNOTES

1. In 2022, UNESCO listed Western Armenian as an endangered language. See https://www.theguardian.com/news/datablog/2011/apr/15/language-extinct-endangered. There have been numerous public and scholarly initiatives over the past two decades to promote Western Armenian language attainment – notably the Calouste Gulbenkian Foundation's funded projects, which include the present volume. Many Armenians who wish to learn Western Armenian often do so now for the very first time at a university. However, there are still prestigious universities with Armenian Studies programs whose language instruction offerings do not fulfill their purported aims, such as, in one instance for example, by appointing an unqualified Armenian language instructor with limited knowledge of Armenian. Such appointments are sadly not uncommon where the personal interests of (almost always male) senior faculty members are concerned. Similarly, there have also been instances of

purported translations from Western Armenian into English – the facts of which simply do not support that claim.

2. See Jillian Tamaki, "The Turkish Novelist Elif Shafak Wants You to Read More Women," Interview with Elif Shafak, *The New York Times*, December 26, 2019, accessed February 16, 2023, https://www.nytimes.com/2019/12/26/books/review/elif-shafak-by-the-book-interview.html.

3. The University of Armenia has made much of Yessayan's writings available on its Digilib.com site. See https://digilib.aua.am/am/ԶԱՊԵԼ%20ԵՍԱՅԵԱՆ/library/549. While valuable, these transcriptions are often riddled with spelling and copy editing errors and are inadequate sources for scholarly work. Some digitized translations of Yessayan's works are also available on Scribd.com.

4. See Nanor Kebranian, "Introduction" in *Captive Nights: From the Bosphorus to Gallipoli* with Zabel Yessayan, Ed. Nanor Kebranian, Trans. G. M. Goshgarian (Fresno: California State UP, 2022): ix – xxvii.

5. See Marc Nichanian, *Writers of Disaster: Armenian Literature in the Twentieth Century* (London: Gomidas Institute, 2002).

6. Zabel Yessayan, "The Newest Manifestation of the Women's Cause," Trans. Nanore Barsoumian in *My Soul in Exile and Other Writings*, Ed. Barbara Merguerian (Boston: AIWA Press, 2014) 83.

7. Yessayan, "Newest," 84.

8. Yessayan, "Newest," 83. Oddly, many of Yessayan's most feminist writings – that is, works that address feminism directly and in a sustained fashion – do not appear in edited volumes of translations presenting her 'feminist' perspectives. These include, notably, the 2006 edited volume, *Bir Adalet Feryadı* [A Cry for Justice], which presented Turkish translations of five women feminist authors produced by a team of 13 editors, translators, and commentators. The section on Yessayan includes seven translated pieces, which do not reflect her deeper feminist engagements or are entirely tangential (e.g. "Düsap ve Tovmas Terzyan" ["Diusap and Tovmas Terzyan"], an excerpt from Yessayan's 1935 autobiographical work, *The Gardens of Silihdar*; or "Meşrutiyet'ten Sonra Ermeni Kadını" ["Armenian Women after the Constitution"]). See *Bir Adalet Feryadı: Osmanlıdan Türkiye'ye Beş Ermeni Feminist Yazar (1862 – 1933)*, Eds. Lerna Ekmekçioğlu and Melissa Bilal (Istanbul: Aras Yayıncılık, 2006). Several extremely important and informative pieces – notably "The Women's Issue" ["Gnotch Hartsë"], "For Peace" ["Khaghaghutyan Hamar"], and "The Role of Armenian Women in Founding Societies" ["Hay Gnotch Terë ir Gazmagerbadz Ëngerutyants Metch"], to name a few –, which provide deeper insights into Yessayan's theoretical, institutional, and

internationalist feminist engagements have been omitted. These pieces are available on Digilib.com, notably the pages, "The Women's Section" ["Ganants Pazhinë] and "For the Fatherland" ["Hayrenikin Hamar"]. See https://digilib.aua.am/book/3752/Հայ%20կինը and https://digilib.aua.am/book/3705/Հայրենիքին%20համար. "For Peace" – not to be confused with the 1911 essay, "Women for Peace" ["Ginë Khaghaghutyan Hamar"] – was published in *Arevelyan Mamul* [Oriental Press], (Smyrna) in 1906. See Zabel Yessayan, "Khaghaghutyan Hamar," *Arevelyan Mamul* (Smyrna), No. 22 (1906): 524 – 527.

9. Zabel Yessayan, "Gnoch Hartsë," *Dzaghig* (Flower, Constantinople), No. 11 (550), April 12, 1903: 125 – 126.

10. Yessayan, "Khaghaghutyan," 526 – 527.

11. Yessayan, "Gnoch Hartsë," 3

12. Zabel Yessayan, "Ginë Khaghaghutyan Hamar," *Arakadz* (New York), No. 3, June 8, 1911: 35–36.

13. Zabel Yessayan, "Hay Gnotch Terë ir Gazmagerbadz Ёngerutyants Metch," *Arakadz* (New York), No. 6, June 26, 1911, 83.

14. Zabel Yessayan, "Our Women Teachers," in *My Soul in Exile and Other Writings*, Trans. Jennifer Manoukian, Ed. Barbara Merguerian (Boston: AIWA, 2014) 78 – 81.

15. Taner Akçam, *Siyasɪ Kültürümüzde Zulüm ve Işkence* (Istanbul: Iletişim, 1992) 300 – 301.

16. Fatma Müge Göçek, *Denial of Violence: Ottoman Past, Turkish Present, and Collective Violence against the Armenians 1789–2009* (New York: OUP, 2015) 137.

17. Göçek, *Denial*, 123.

18. Selim Deringil, "Conversion as Survival: Mass Conversions of Armenians in Anatolia, 1895 – 1897" *in Conversion and Apostasy in the Late Ottoman Empire* (Cambridge: Cambridge UP, 2012) 197 – 239.

19. Nanor Kebranian, "Imprisoned Communities: Punishing Politics in the Late Ottoman Empire" in *Ottoman-Armenians Vol. 1: Life, Culture, Society*, Ed. Vahé Tachjian (Berlin: Houshamadyan, 2014) 115 – 143.

20. Unfortunately, despite the abundant available evidence, histories of late Ottoman prisons have treated these facts as 'salacious accounts' amounting to 'hyperbole – products of those with clear political agendas.' See Kent Schull, *Prisons in the Late Ottoman Empire: Microcosms of Modernity* (Edinburgh: Edinburgh UP, 2014) 147. See also Göçek, *Denial*, 124. Based on the dubious accounts in two 19th century Muslim officials' memoirs, Göçek concludes inaccurately, "[T]hose opposing the sultan's rule or protesting the injustices [i.e. 'revolutionaries'] they encountered *were, upon being caught, often pardoned*" (emphasis added). There is plenty

of counterevidence to contradict these Muslim officials' accounts and Göçek's assessment. Moreover, this statement does not account for the fact that just because such prisoners were 'pardoned,' they were therefore unharmed or that their release demonstrates the state's tolerance or leniency. A significant proportion of prisoners was subjected to horrific deprivations and tortures, often emerging from their incarceration with irreparable physical and mental injuries. See Kebranian, "Imprisoned Communities." See also, Akçam, *Siyası Kültürümüzde Zulüm ve Işkence*. In one salient example, Akçam recounts the arrest of 50 Armenians after an uprising in Merzifon. Seven were sentenced to death, but 'only' five executed thanks to Western pressure. The state was more than willing to exert the full force of its justice system to eliminate its Armenian opponents, whenever practically and diplomatically possible.

21. Arpiar Arpiarian, *Badmutyun XIX Taru Turkyo Hayots Kraganutyan* [History of 19th century Armenian Literature in Turkey] (Cairo: Hussaper, 1944) 75.

22. Arpiarian, *Badmutyun*, 75.

23. Teotig, *Dib u Dar* [Print and Letter] (Constantinople: Vahram and Hratch Der Nersesian, 1912) 105.

24. Known as the 'Zeytun Rebellion,' this event marked a momentous turning point for Ottoman-Armenians. Using the pretext of local disputes, the Ottoman army attacked and leveled the Armenian village of Alabash and then proceeded to attempt the same in Zeytun while laying Armenian properties to ruin along the way. An irregular Armenian fighting force – aided by local Muslims – comprising around 5,000 men successfully defended Zeytun against an army of 40,000. But this merely inflamed the state's resolve to quash the Zeytun Armenians, and the locals resorted to diplomacy via the Armenian Istanbul community and with the support of French intervention to avert another assault. See Louise Nalbandian, *The Armenian Revolutionary Movement: The Development of Armenian Political Parties through the Nineteenth Century* (Berkeley: University of California, 1963) 70 – 74. This event remarkably eludes Göçek's study, *Denial of Violence*, which incorrectly asserts that "the first wave of violence committed against the Armenians" consisted of incidents that took place in the early 1890s during Abdülhamid II's rule. See Göçek, 131. The first time Zeytun is mentioned in the work is with reference to the 'rebellion' of 1893. It is sometimes difficult to accurately gauge progressive Turkish and/ or Ottoman Studies scholars' interpretations of the Ottoman-Armenian experience, including the genocide. I once attended an invited lecture at Columbia University during which one leading Turkish scholar who seemed to conclude that Ottoman-Armenians underwent a genocide

nonetheless asserted that 'it sort of happened;' namely, that it was not intended or planned. Puzzled by this claim, a few scholars in attendance objected, since the definition of genocide as a crime is premised on the indispensable element of intent to destroy a people in whole or in part on the basis of their religion, ethnicity, nationality, or race. See "Convention on the Prevention and Punishment of the Crime of Genocide," UN.org, accessed February 20, 2023, https://www.un.org/en/genocideprevention/documents/atrocity-crimes/Doc.1_Convention%20on%20the%20Prevention%20and%20Punishment%20of%20the%20Crime%20of%20Genocide.pdf.

25. Leo, "Mgrditch Beshigtashlian" in Mgrditch Beshigtashlian, *Dagher* [Verses] (Tiflis: Vrats, 1903) 22.

26. Teotig, *Dib*, 105.

27. These works' oversight stems mainly from a crisis of inadequate research and an over-reliance on Chouchik Dasnabédian's incomplete and frequently inaccurate bibliography of Zabel Yessayan. See Chouchik Dasnabédian, *Zabel Essayan ou l'univers lumineux de la littérature* (Antelias: Armenian Catholicosate of Cilicia, 1988). One noted Armenian 'feminist' scholar asserted in conversation with me some years ago that she had read 'everything' written by Yessayan as compiled by Dasnabédian. Based on my own findings, I assured her that the list was incomplete. Regardless, her claim was simply not tenable, given that the bibliography's various mistaken citations often lead to numerous dead ends, rendering it impossible to find and read every item on Dasnabédian's list. This is true specifically of Yessayan's publications in periodicals. Given Dasnabédian's errors, one must often conduct painstaking archival research among those periodicals to locate the proper sources.

28. Judith Butler, *The Psychic Life of Power: Theories in Subjection* (Stanford: Stanford UP, 1997).

29. Nanor Kebranian, "Lost in Conversion: Mourning the Armenian-Turk," *Middle Eastern Literatures* 17(3) (2014): 238 – 262.

30. Julia Duin, "Islam's 'Idealistic Version of Itself' Not Quite the Reality," Interview with Bat Ye'or, *The Washington Times* (Washington D.C.), October 30, 2002, A14, accessed February 17, 2023, link.gale.com/apps/doc/A93607069/STND?u=nantecun&sid=bookmark-STND&xid=ee668b41. *The Washington Times* is a conservative daily newspaper that was previously owned by the South Korean founder of the controversial Unification Church, a new Christian religious movement.

31. Ekmekçioğlu employs the term without indicating its source or identifying its scholarly coinage by Bat Ye'or. In fact, she seems to employ the term as though it were her own coinage. See its repeated uncritical and

uncited usage throughout her book, *Recovering Armenia: The Limits of Belonging in Post-Genocide Turkey* (Stanford: Stanford UP, 2016) 42; 166 – 168; 172; 178; 195.

32. See Andrew Brown, "The Myth of Eurabia: How a Far-Right Conspiracy Theory Went Mainstream," *The Guardian*, August 16, 2019, https://www.theguardian.com/world/2019/aug/16/the-myth-of-eurabia-how-a-far-right-conspiracy-theory-went-mainstream, accessed February 17, 2023.

33. I have commented on such shortcomings in Marc Nichanian's study of Hagop Oshagan, *Le Roman de la Catastrophe: Entre l'art et le témoignage* (Geneva: MétisPresses, 2008). See Kebranian, "Mourning." Krikor Beledian approaches the issue in his essay on Realist short stories, but extremely narrowly and with very little contextualization. See Krikor Beledian, "Noravebë yev Kerutyunë" ["The Short Story and Captivity"], *Mard* (Antelias: Catholicosate of Cilicia, 1997) 70 - 73.

34. Armenian historiography treads a precarious road if it fails to acknowledge the centrality of linguistic proficiency in producing adequate scholarship. Appointing scholars without Armenian language literacy as professors of Armenian history at major universities only diminishes the field. Armenian historiography also suffers a disservice from histories presented through inadequate archival research or masquerading as something they are not. Is a history based primarily on a single periodical with a questionably feminist editor (Haiganush Mark) really a history of post-genocide Armenians in the Ottoman Empire/Turkey? I may not be the first to pose that query. See Nazan Maksudyan, "Review of Lerna Ekmekçioğlu, Recovering Armenia: The Limits of Belonging in Post-Genocide Turkey," *New Perspectives on Turkey* 55 (2014): 136-140. One does wonder about the peer review processes being employed by current major university press editors publishing histories of Ottoman-Armenians. As for Haiganush Mark, see Vahé Tachjian's knowledgeable assessment of her dubious feminism: Vahé Tachjian, "Mixed Marriage, Prostitution, Survival: Reintegrating Armenian Women into Post-Ottoman Cities" in *Women and the City, Women in the City: A Gendered Perspective on Ottoman Urban History*, Ed. Nazan Maksudyan (New York: Berghahn, 2014) 94; and note 20 regarding Ekmekçioğlu's misleading inversion of Mark's racist and counter-feminist discourse as evidence of the contrary. The consistently racist Mark once referred to Yessayan as using a "somewhat Jewish way of bargaining" when the latter asked to be paid for the written work that Mark had requested of her for her newly founded periodical, *Dzaghig*. Mark wrote, "What disappointed me in Zabel Yesayan on that day was that somewhat Jewish way of her bargaining for honorarium when

at stake was a woman's magazine which was being founded with no preliminary budget and for the sake of an ideal." See Hasmig Khalapyan, "Armenian Women's Writing in the Ottoman Empire, Late 19th to Early 20th Centuries," EVN Report, March 12, 2019, https://evnreport.com/raw-unfiltered/armenian-womens-writing-in-the-ottoman-empire-late-19th-to-early-20th-centuries/ accessed February 28, 2023. As Khalapyan comments, "These words, coming from Mark, a woman who spent the longest years in journalism, leave the reader with the impression that Mark herself for years worked for the sake of ideals only." Recently, Vartouhie Calantar Nalbandian has also been receiving undue attention as a notable Armenian woman, despite her similarly racist discourse. This was brought to my attention during a presentation – "Cerberus's Many Heads: Ethnoreligious Entanglements and Uncommon Kinships on the Women's Block of Constantinople's Central Prison" – by UPenn doctoral student, Deanna Cachoian-Schanz for a panel I organized – "Comparative Perspectives on Forced Displacement, Religion, and Communal Reconstruction among Minorities of the Middle East (20th - 21st Centuries)" – at the 2022 European Academy of Religions conference in Bologna. Calantar's prison memoir, *Getronagan Pandi Ginerun Pazhinë* [The Women's Block of the Central Prison] was published by Aras Yayıncılık in Istanbul (2022) and is replete with numerous instances of racial stereotyping and counter-feminist statements. Moreover, this memoir has been falsely declared by Ekmekçioğlu as "the only known first person narrative of an Ottoman prisoner" in an announcement – presumably partly penned by her – for her public lecture on Calantar's book. See the announcement for the talk organized by the National Association of Armenian Studies and Research (NAASR) held online on September 22, 2021 and entitled, "The Political Mademoiselle of the Women's Ward: Vartouhi Calantar-Nalbandian at Istanbul's Central Prison (1915 – 18)," https://naasr.org/blogs/events-1/the-political-mademoiselle-of-the-women-s-ward-vartouhie-calantar-nalbandian-at-istanbul-s-central-prison-1915-18-wednesday-september-22-2021-on-zoom-youtube, accessed February 17, 2023. Ekmekçioğlu's introduction to Calantar's book also falsely claims, "Generally all the writings we know of concerning Ottoman prisons have reached us through the reports of functionaries or outside observers." See Calantar, *Getronagan*, 9. And she also falsely claims that Misak Kochunyan's (1863 – 1913) novel, *Gragin Mechen* [Through the Fire] (Yerevan: Dikran Medz, 2010) is his prison memoir. See Calantar, *Getronagan*, note 7. On that same page, she claims to have found a prison memoir by the renowned poet, Vahan Tekeyan, in which he appears to have been imprisoned in 1902. She incorrectly claims that this was an imprisonment of two *months*, whereas the narrative indicates two *weeks*. However, the authenticity of this piece as a memoir per se remains to be corroborated. As per Tekeyan's biographers, the writer left the Empire in 1896, not to return until 1908. Therefore, it is entirely possible that this is a fictional piece, especially as a) it omits any details confirming the narrator's identity as Tekeyan himself or further particulars regarding the reasons for his arrest and release; and b) the narrative concludes by suggesting that the narrator may have imagined all this. See Vahan Tekeyan, "Pandeghpayrnerë (Hishadagner)" ["Prison Brothers (Memories)"], *Shirag* (Constantinople), August 1, 1909, No. 21, p. 528. Furthermore, this is not the first or only piece by Tekeyan to be published as a prison reminiscence. A few months earlier, he published a piece entitled, "Destanë: Pandi Hishadagner" ["The Epic: Memories from Prison"]. However, this too omits any autobiographical information, indicating that it might be a fictional account inspired by contemporaneous prison memoirs, while contesting their primary themes. See Vahan Tekeyan, "Destanë: Pandi Hishadagner" ["The Epic: Memories from Prison"], *Shirag* (Constantinople), February 21, 1909, No. 3, pp. 49 – 56. Most importantly, Ekmekçioğlu's statement regarding the dearth of Ottoman-Armenian prison memoirs either exercises a willful omission or constitutes an egregious oversight. It would benefit Armenian historiography tremendously were its practitioners to enact the basic principles of academic integrity by producing truthful, transparent, authentic, well-founded, and fair scholarship. Contrary to Ekmekçioğlu's false claims, my 2010 doctoral dissertation at Oxford University uncovered numerous Ottoman-Armenian prison memoirs, published both in periodicals and as separate volumes, as well as numerous significant literary works – including the epic historical novel, *Pande Pand* [Prison to Prison] by Smpad Piurad, who had been entirely forgotten until my rediscovery, despite having been immensely popular in his time. My doctorate also presented a genealogy of these works' transmission and commented on their significance. Many other entirely unknown memoirs have surfaced in my continued research into this previously uncharted field in Ottoman-Armenian historiography during my preparation for a book-length study of Ottoman-Armenian political imprisonment. See my other findings and elaborations about the Ottoman-Armenian prison experience in my aforenoted chapter, "Imprisoned Communities"; my article, "Beyond 'the Armenian': Literature, Revolution, Ideology and Hagop Oshagan's Haji Murat," *Journal of the Society for Armenian Studies* 19(2), 2010: 117 – 146; and my introduction to Oshagan's *Remnants*, Trans. G. M. Goshgarian (London: Gomidas Institute, 2013).

35. I once attended a faculty seminar at Columbia University in which a senior scholar of the Middle East presented a paper where he mentioned the use of 'bribery' in an Islamic state. He was translating the term from the Arabic as used by a local Arab Muslim. A prominent scholar of Islam was in attendance and insisted that the term did not have the same connotations as its English equivalent; and that bribery was an accepted form of social transaction in the noted context. When this was rationally rebutted by the presenting scholar who explained that the local Arab Muslim dissident was employing 'bribery' as part of a broader critical discourse, the scholar of Islam resorted to shouting, "I was almost killed!" It was a hyper-emotional non-sequitur referring to his own erstwhile persecution as an Arab Muslim. Naturally, the outburst silenced any further discussion on the matter. The rest of us were left to draw our own conclusions on whether 'bribery' exists in Islamic societies.

36. Edward W. Saïd, *Culture and Imperialism* (New York: Vintage, 1994) xxii.

37. Specifically the line, "Am I indeed Armenian, whereas you, Armenia, are not mine" ["Միթէ Հա՞յ եմ մինչդեռ չես իմ, Հայաստա՛ն"]. Bedros Tourian, *Kertvadzner* (Poems) (Beirut: Hraztan, 1926) 28.

38. Tourian, *Kertvadzner*, 21–22.

39. Oddly, Beledian identifies "Kaghtagannerë" ["The Refugees"] and "Hasmignerë" ["The Jasmines"] as such related stories, but not the more directly relevant ones noted by me here. See Beledian, *Mard*, 168.

40. Marc Nichanian, "Catastrophic Mourning" in *Loss: The Politics of Mourning*, Eds. David L. Eng and David Kazanjian (Berkeley: University of California, 2003) 107.

41. Krikor Beledian, "Zabel Yessayan Averagnerun Mech" ["Zabel Yessayan in the Ruins"] in *Mard* (Antelias: Catholicosate of Cilicia, 1997) 167 – 193. Beledian's essay provides the first real engagement with Yessayan's chronicle, although it is almost never cited. All subsequent readings, including Nichanian's, owe much of their findings to that essay, even when that fact is not made duly evident.

42. Nichanian, "Catastrophic," 101.

43. Nichanian, "Catastrophic," 101.

44. Zabel Yessayan, *Averagnerun Mech* [In the Ruins] (Istanbul: Aras, 2010) 36.

45. Yessayan, *Ruins*, 36 – 37.

46. Nichanian, "Catastrophic," 105.

47. Yessayan, *Averag*, 34.

48. Yessayan, *Averag*, 34.

49. Yessayan, *Averag*, 34.

50. Nichanian, "Catastrophic," 105.

51. The word is capitalized, hence meaning, "Aryan." In lower case, the same word could also mean, "brave, heroic." Yessayan, *Averag*, 80.

52. Cengiz Aktar, "Confronting Past Violence with More Violence," *Ahval*, December 31, 2017, https://ahvalnews.com/armenians/confronting-past-violence-more-violence#, accessed February 20, 2023.

53. Léon Kétcheyan, "Zabel Essayan (1878 – 1943): sa vie et on temps. Traduction annotée de l'autobiographie et de la correspondance," Doctoral Dissertation, March 30, 2002, École Pratique des Hautes Études (Paris) 66.

54. Yessayan, "On the Question of Turkish Women's Emancipation."

Zabel Yessayan on the Threshold:

Key Texts on Armenians and Turks as Ottoman Subjects

2.b.

The *Yashmak:*[*] On Life in the Orient

"Yes, I love you, the loveliest girl in your land. I love you, and my smoldering heart is a fistful of embers. You, my master's favorite, you mastered my soul. And I am now a rudderless ship, adrift on the open sea. I am a wingless bird that yearns to soar, but that yearning drowns within me…"

"I love you, and that is why I stole your *yashmak*."

The eunuch clenched a white veil to his breast and then lifted it to his eyes, but they were dry, burdened, oppressed by an aching to weep. He doffed his red fez and pressed his face to the ground, remaining prostrate for the few moments when his mind composed this verse:

"You fluttered like a butterfly into the flowerbed of my lord's estate. Not once did your deep almond-shaped eyes smile, and the autumnal flower of your lips never broke into song. Why those dew-soaked lashes? Why all those tearful sighs, those precious pearls which I would gather every time I entered your chambers? But your anguish only deepens your beauty and compels my love to grow. At night, when your voice subsides and your fragrance is all that wafts through the hallways, when the flower of your figure vanishes from the divans, I shall be alone no more. With your *yashmak* upon my heart, I shall think of you, and search its folds for the traces of your divine head."

The eunuch strained painfully to raise his head. Chamlija cast an enormous shadow over the sun-scorched lawn, which assumed a cerulean hue as it sank into the shade. Here and there, rigid crags in the scarlet earth appeared ready to erupt. Beetles hung motionless in midair, as though they were struck by sudden paralysis. And, in the distance, sunstruck passersby staggered like drunkards.

Smothering his passion within his coal-black eyes, the eunuch got to his feet and stood perfectly straight. His skin glistened with a metallic sheen, and his eyes blazed with a bluish flame. Engorged with blood, his full violet lips dropped onto his chin, and his nostrils flared even wider. He reached the long black boughs of his fingers uneasily to his hair, and

[*]. A veil worn by women to cover most of the face, except for the eyes. (Tr.)

after erecting the whole length of his slender body upwards, he walked away with heavy steps.

Twilight cast its golden rays. They beamed through the narrow slits between the crossbars and onto the pink satin divans, gradually fading away. The carpets brightened with the vivid tones of meadows in bloom, while the exotic plants in the corner extended their graceful leaves out of violet vases.

Sayid Bey was seated in one corner of the divan. His silk yellow *entari** cascaded from his shoulders down to the floor, flowing into long folds, and his broad sleeves dangled from forearms that weighed heavy with the large amber stones of his prayer beads. Leaning against the gold-threaded cushions, he occasionally brought his nargileh's amber tip slowly to his lips, and the room filled with a melodious, muffled gurgling along with the fragrance of *tembeki.*†

Before him, Zekiya Hanum lay supine on a tiger-skin rug. Her almond-shaped black eyes were drowning in sorrow, and her lips were pale and taciturn. She was resting her head on a cushion and her pitch-black hair coiled over her supple shoulders. A diamond star pinned her curls to her forehead, and her shoulders seemed to buckle beneath the chains of pearls that looped from her neck down to her chest. Her tiny feet peeked through her white dress, and the tips of her toes could barely hold onto her satin yellow slippers. With apricot-tinted nails and weighed down by rings and bracelets, her hands drooped over her waist.

Sayid Bey spoke to her now and then, "My lovely girl, sing me one of your sweetest tunes. The birds of paradise would die of envy at the sound of your voice, which could beguile even the haughtiest flower. Sing me one of the sweetest songs of your land."

And her voice rose like a lament in the oppressive room, "A strange pain torments me..."

The melody steadily swelled, permeating the stifling atmosphere, and then collapsed mournfully into the chorus, "Each day adds to my grief..."

---

*. A robe-like garment worn over clothing. (Tr.)
†. A type of tobacco used in nargilehs. (Tr.)

Dismayed, Sayid Bey told her, "May the sun that witnessed the day you entered this world be blessed, may the milk that nourished your majesty be blessed... But can you tell me, Zekiya, why is it that you cannot smile? No matter, I derive more delight from your languid movements as you sway with the grace of a rosebush in the breeze. Where is your *yashmak*? Put it on, cover your face with that veil, the one embroidered just for you by the fairies of India, the one that adorns you the way that white clouds adorn the moon..."

Sayid Bey paused briefly. But then his lips flushed with an adoring smile, "Go on, you exquisite girl, veil your face with that *yashmak*, put on your violet *ferajeh*[*] and come this way as if you are a butterfly taking flight... I shall catch you like a bird that has fled from its cage... I shall hold your body, weightless as the breeze, captive in my arms, but – and this is important – you must not forget your *yashmak*."

Motionless, and with her head slumped onto her shoulder, Zekiya gently replied, "My lord, your wish is my sacred command, but I cannot possibly do as you wish. I have lost my *yashmak*."

Sayid Bey failed to hear her, "The *yashmak* that flutters like a zephyr across your face, that was embroidered for you by the fairies of India ..."

Outside the mansion, the eunuch stood in the dark and ruminated. Passion coursed quietly through his whole body, and his widowed soul, forsaken by tenderness, wasted away, fading into the night. A mysterious force had conjured a storm in his blood, and his entire being ached with longing; a longing for a distant receding horizon, for a world of total grief and sorrow, which he had never known but which foolishly troubled him.

"Oh Gloom, Envoy of the afflicted and consumptive, a strange fever burns in my soul, while I, like you, await the break of day. But, for me, day never breaks. Tell the one I worship that my face is and will always be black. May my tears moisten her tracks, may my heart ignite like an offering and be reduced to ashes for her."

Before him, beyond the straits, the light-drenched city stretched into the night, cloaked in an air of decadence and intoxication. The wind passed over him, carrying echoes of kisses and the sighs of lovesick

---

*. A long coat worn by women. (Tr.)

hearts. As though he were dreaming, he thought he was being surrounded by creatures that refused to materialize before his delirious eyes. A morbid anxiety sent shivers through him, and, as his limbs tightened, they forced him to his feet. He stood as tall as the cypresses in the cemetery. His black features vanished into his lengthening shadow. He felt as if he had been brought to the very brink of life and forgotten there. And as he raised hands that would never receive solace, his whole sickly being released a futile appeal into the void. Yet, life continued to flow with all its charms and enticements, enveloping him, at times even touching his lips, suffocating him with its sultry embrace, but his parched soul refused every drop.

His wet lashes drooped and shut like a coffin, entombing a soul that was destined to become a pile of bones. And it seemed to him that he was nothing but a shadow, that he did not exist. And he felt nothing within him but the two cold teardrops that pierced his cheeks like a pair of nails.

The mansion's residents were fast asleep when the eunuch entered the premises. He went without heed towards the chambers of his mistress and crouched on the threshold behind her door.

Sayid Bey was away, and Zekiya was in her room, dreaming with her head buried in the pillows. As though something were sending shivers up her spine, sometimes her whole body would begin to quake. And she would raise her small head for a moment to survey her surroundings nervously. She could hear sobs behind her door.

Unable to sleep, she got up and demanded tetchily, "Who's at my door?"

"Gloom is at your door, and he weeps," murmured the eunuch. "You, who embody light, scorn it, but a tempest is brewing in the gloom...."

All Zekiya heard was a faint sound and then the footsteps of someone walking away.

Sayid Bey finally learned about the eunuch's peculiar secret, and, in his outrage, pale with envy, he thought up the most terrible punishments. When they found Zekiya's lost *yashmak* in the eunuch's breast pocket, Sayid Bey's heart hardened, and he ordered his men to strangle the culprit.

Over the next three days, passersby could see the black man's body swaying from the scaffold. His eyes were bulging, and the skin on his face had cracked. And for three days, the *yashmak*, the same *yashmak* that had received so many of his tears and whose folds he had showered with kisses of such longing and passion, remained ringed round his neck, after strangling him like the bonds of fate.

Տիկին ԶԱՊԷԼ ԵՍԱՅԵԱՆ

His Hate

Why did that man hate me, why…? It has already been two months since that horrible incident and even during my most distressing days and throughout my long recovery, everyone persisted in posing the same question… As though, somehow, I had an answer, as though I could explain why, why that man hated me.

Why…? I have posed the very same question from the depths of my troubled heart and soul. What had I done? How had it been possible for me to stir the pits of this man's hate? A man whom I hardly knew and who had no reason to see me as his nemesis.

We first met at my friend's house. He was tall, dark-complexioned, and taciturn. He bowed his head slowly when my friend made the requisite introductions. And as I extended my hand with a smile, my eyes met his, those black, implacably stern eyes. That is when I sensed that this man hated me.

Why…? I cannot possibly say. Had we already met? Or did I somehow awaken an excruciating passion that had lain dormant within him…? Did I resemble someone who had tormented him endlessly, who had cloaked his ominous figure with fits of agony? For, there were noticeable wrinkles of sorrow along his mouth, on his temples, because his forehead was almost creased with pleats of anguish and his entire being – taciturn, stern, and morose – harbored something unnerving and contemptuous against all and sundry.

All this I recall clearly, distinctly now in the ennui of my interminable recovery, all this, ah, and I wonder how I had not been able to suspect him from the very start.

Because back then, I fell under the spell of his cruel unforgiving eyes and despite the fear that he instilled in me, I felt an indescribable pull towards him and – all this is true – towards his sinister black gaze.

And yet I sensed that this man felt profound hatred for me. I knew that his hatred had been brewing within his soul like a veritable tempest, uncontrollable, all-consuming. And when he was obliged to reach his pale fingers towards mine, constricting them painfully, oh, I knew all too well that they were chilled by feelings of rage and suppressed violence.

Not a soul around me noticed a thing. He sealed himself off like a grave in their presence. And their only comment was that he was generally an unpleasant man; that was all.

One day, I was visiting my friend at her home, when He entered the salon. Weeks had passed without sight of him. And, for weeks, that pitiless man had been tormented by the prospect of encountering me. Assuming that I would be there, he had elected to stay away, choosing to spare me the poison of his vile malevolent gaze... Because... I have mentioned that an inexplicable, mad, pathological feeling had slithered into my soul like a snake. I cannot explain why I yearned to place myself beneath that gaze, to feel my bright blue irises fade into the shadows of his eyes. An experience tantamount to rape, when a tumult of emotions overtook my soul and compelled it towards the unknown and harrowing horizons of ecstasy.

I could sense how his long sharp teeth had a craving for my flesh, and this made me quake with hitherto unknown tremors... At last!... What had possessed his black turbid soul? I cannot say. Only, He decidedly shunned my presence. My friend told me all this in revealing detail. She told me that He had made himself scarce wherever I might happen to be, wherever I might be a topic of conversation, and they had all assumed that this was provoked by an unreciprocated fondness... Fondness...? Ah, but I knew how that man hated me. I knew that my diminutive, inconspicuous, youthful being awakened a storm of hatred and passion in his soul. Oh, what features marked my skin, what did his eyes encounter in my bright pupils that made him grimace painfully as though something had suddenly stung him? And his fingers would tense tightly with an unfulfilled yearning for brute violence.

But all at once, that day He appeared in the salon. It was still very early, and I was alone. My friend was busy getting dressed for the evening in the boudoir next door. I was seated at the table with my back to the door as I leafed through some newspapers. It was Him. I could sense that it was Him... And it was then and only then that I felt unease and fear. I felt that being alone with him placed me in great irrevocable danger... I dared not turn my head and pretending to be preoccupied, I bent my head even lower over the papers... And ah... Just above my collar on the nape of my neck, I had the sensation of something indescribably cold. Was it his hand? Or already the cold surface of metal or perhaps... Oh... I sprang up and saw him standing behind me, his hands in his pockets, extremely pale and shaking. A few drops of sweat ran down his temples and his eyes revealed a firm resolve to destroy, a fleeting black flame that darkened his brow and filled his gaze with something strange and sinister. I was about to scream like a woman possessed; I was going to flee when my friend entered the room. Heaven knows what impression we made as we stood there trembling and anxious that her lips broke into a little smile and, as she took my icy hands into hers, she kissed me warmly and murmured something into my ear which I only heard as a jumble of noise. As for him? Oh... That stern peculiar man had dropped into an armchair looking weary and dejected, still vaguely trembling. And his incessantly twitching face altered his expression entirely.

As my bewildered friend looked on, he approached me, reluctantly, with eyes closed as though he were blind, and his lips pursed so tautly that they revealed the outline of his long sharp teeth through his black moustache. Then a door slammed. When the new visitors entered the salon, He had vanished. But I knew from that moment on that, step by step, I was advancing towards the inevitable. I felt that I was going through the long and agonizing throes of death and that my days were numbered. Those eyes did not lie, murder lurked in those eyes... My life turned into a prolonged martyrdom, unbearable, excruciating, fitful. Anxious with fear and suspicion, I could not walk through the streets, because I was terrorized by the sound of a man's footsteps behind me.

Because he was indeed pursuing me, because his menacing eyes were fixed on me, spying on my every move, because his black soul, his hate-filled soul thirsted for my life...

Months had gone by, and I had begun to regain some hope as I recuperated. Little by little the memory of his ominous silhouette was being erased from my mind and ceased to possess me. My *joie-de-vivre* returned and brought the rosiness back to my perpetually sleepless face. And were it not for the dark circles around my eyes, no one would have suspected my long months of agony... Ah, I did not know that his spirit, his noxious spirit, had permeated my surroundings. How had He done it, hiding like a common villain? How had he been able to contemplate his crime for days on end and with such astonishing *sang-froid*, as though he were accustomed to that line of work... When all these things come to mind, I feel as though I am standing once more on that staircase, and his long fingers, his fiendish frigid fingers begin to press into my neck...

And so, I was slowly coming back to life, when one evening after returning from a visit with a relative who saw me to my door, I began mounting the staircase... I stopped at once. It was Him... In the dark. I could not see a thing, but I felt Him there, standing tall a few steps above me. I froze in an instant and remember nothing else now with any clarity... Only fragments of faint sensations come back to me. I pulled myself up at once and my dress fell open at the chest. Ah, it was horrible, monstrous... And then just as I felt him grip me in his long, sinewy arms, a strange noise... Dull and loud, which seemed to come from afar, quite far, when I felt what seemed to be a lightning bolt strike my skull, and my whole brain swiftly lit up with an indescribable flash... And then a tiny drop, water dripping into a hollow, followed by darkness... darkness... darkness...

They found me there in a pitiful state with a large gash on my temple. And, for several days, my life hung from a thread. As for him?... They found him at home dazed, staring, and unresponsive. They say that ever since, he has remained that way in his cell, still dazed, refusing to eat, to speak, to sleep, his eyes riveted on the same spot, always, motionless, for hours on end...

Now that I have almost fully recovered, and now that I must offer some sort of explanation that can satisfy both the judges and society at large as to why, why that man hated me, what can I say? It is a question that haunts my impaired brain, that torments me. Perhaps even He, as he sits staring in his cell, questions the nature of his deranged, demented feelings.

And I believe that if I retold this story from the very beginning, sparing no detail and adhering to the absolute truth, people would understand why He hated me.

The Curse

The day had just dawned, and a rosy radiance pressed ahead from the eastern skies. Wisps of yellowish violet clouds fled westward from the advancing light. The deep green tips of myrtle trees thrust through a bluish mist and quivered with a distant, barely audible rustle. A dense patch of poplars gently swayed, and between their trunks stretched tranquil plains that vanished into the line on the horizon.

The village of Charpunar was already awake, but a somber, almost deathly stillness weighed heavily upon it. Flimsy plumes of smoke, thin and tremulous, rose from a few chimneys here and there. The majestic, imperious morning light dawned over the village but seemed not to penetrate it.

Everyone in the village head's household was awake before daylight, because policemen on horseback had arrived from the city to arrest his youngest son, Habib. Purely by chance, Habib had left the village the previous day to search for work in the nearby cotton fields; and that is why the police had returned emptyhanded.

At that moment, the household's daughters and daughters-in-law were overcome with fear. They had neglected their housework and congregated in a corner to speak at length about the terrifying and inconceivable news that they had been hearing.

The village head, an eighty-year-old man wearing a white *entari* and a linen cap sat cross-legged on his mat and was immersed in thought. His weak elderly eyes were even blearier than usual and seemed to be losing their remaining light behind the white web of his prominent long eyebrows. Occasionally, his beard fluttered over his chest, and when he spoke, his eyes seemed to follow his meandering thoughts. His skeletal body, stiff with the dread of what he had heard, had withered still more beneath his *entari*'s folds.

What had it all come to, living to see all this before closing his eyes for the final sleep? Brothers turning on each other... oooph.... ooph...

His elderly wife, less aged and still lively, was attending to her husband. But the gray-haired old man, who had forgotten his nargileh's pipe on his knees, hadn't once brought it up to his pale shriveled lips, while the *kahveh*[*] on the stool next to him was getting cold.

The first set of gallows had been erected in Adana, when the police had brought them the wretched news. And just as they had snapped out of that nightmarish possibility, they had been informed that a search was on for Habib who had also been sentenced to death by the Military Tribunal.

The soul of the bewildered old man turned bitter. At first, he did not grasp the immensity of the tragedy that had befallen them, but now the truth smarted his heart like an incurable wound. Swells of woeful thoughts collided within him.

"Allah help us… and so, Muslim eyes, wretched eyes, have now seen the bodies of Muslims swaying on the gallows."

His age-stiffened fingers trembled on his knees and with mute, unsteady movements, he reached for his cane. When he found it, he ordered the old woman to take away his nargileh and got to his feet.

At sunrise, the old man sent his three sons to deliver the news to the heads of household, so that they could meet and decide on how to respond to this shocking catastrophe.

The village, once so prosperous and serene, was now the picture of hopeless misfortune; as though evil loomed above it, limitless, like a black cloud. Outside the cottages, beneath the shade of ancient trees, people were drifting around downcast and gloomy. Even the children did not play, did not make a sound, did not gather in groups, and looking even gloomier than the adults, they wandered aimlessly into dark corners making terrifying and indecipherable gestures.

The women stole out of the cottages. Covered with stiff veils, they looked like phantoms. Their slow gait suggested fearful resignation, because all the villagers existed, without pause, day and night, in a nightmare from which they could not wake.

The village head mournfully revisited the events of the recent past. At the outset, the wisdom of old age and Muslim piety had made him reluctant to believe that the crime was officially planned; that shrewd,

---

*. Coffee. (Tr.)

heartless men had ignited the flames of hatred in the hearts of once courageous men, inciting them until the horrific catastrophe had occurred. All the villagers had turned into blind, deaf beasts, senseless and violent, and thirsting for blood... Allah, have mercy on us!...

Suddenly he seemed to grasp the whole terrifying scope of all the evil that had been done, and his entire body shook as he recalled the crime and those frenzied days, when the sky overhead had been reddened by the conflagration of Armenian villages... when those returning from the fighting and carnage had marched for so long through blood that the dusty roads had been unable to purge the crimson stains from the soles of their feet... But today, the hour of retribution was chiming. He saw, as though it were a dream, the gallows erected in Adana and the Muslim bodies swaying pitifully, their eyes bulging out of their sockets and their faces disfigured by infernal contortions...

"They're going to hang Habib!" cried the old man unexpectedly, his voice rough and forceful, and his entire body began to quake.... His thoughts darkened, and stupefied, he looked up at the sky and then across the village rooftops. Unfathomable fatigue engulfed his soul and exhausted, he returned once more to this thought, "I wish that I was blind so that I couldn't see, deaf so that I couldn't hear. I wish my wretched body could leave this lawless land..."

The village head's daughters and daughters-in-law rushed to the roof and struggled to bring the old man to his senses. He saw but could not blink, heard but could not reply, and only the right arm of his palsied body shook, as though it had detached from his torso, pounding the roof all the while with the cane held firmly in its grip.

The sun had risen over the horizon and its rays shot down in every direction, shining on the old man's white *entari* and snowy beard, playing on the movements of the young women, fluttering and shimmering on their hair, dazzling their eyes, even setting alight the buildings of chalk and brick...

Only to the old man's eyes had the sun gently set beneath the dome of Cilicia's skies.

***

A few days had passed since the death of the village head, and Habib's mother was in a state of panic: the police had returned and were insistently demanding to know her son's whereabouts. Habib had not come home, and his mother did not even know whether he might already be in the surrounding villages.

"Where are you, *oghloom?*[*]" she would cry as she beat her thighs with her fists. "Is your head resting on a rock, are you hiding in the shadows? Ah, my heart breaks for you, for your brave soul!"

At first, everyone in the village had shared her pain, but little by little their feelings cooled. They all feared for themselves, because they all felt as guilty as Habib. Their eyes strayed. They became cautious and evasive. Their lips fell silent, because every word that they uttered could have become a confession.

Even inside their own cottages, they felt like they were walking on thorns, as though every plundered object was taking on a life of its own and standing before the murderers in menacing silence. Old women began collecting the *ooghoorsooz*[†] spoils and stashing them in secret cellars. The hands of young men began to tremble, unable to toil; suspicion and fear paralyzed even the most daring among them. And the most horrifying thing of all was that every one of them knew what atrocities their neighbors had committed. In a crazed and bloodthirsty frenzy, they had not only seen each other over the many days of the *zooloom*,[‡] sometimes even *laboring in communion on the same body*, but they had also eagerly shared their stories of underhanded acts. They had bragged about their feats, and they had tried to outdo one another with the unspeakable and unbelievable details of their deeds.

Was it truly possible...? Was that whole ill-fated past not perhaps merely a terrible dream?

"We were wrong, and we were duped," they muttered to their closest kin, and they sensed that they hated one another, because they all saw the reflection of their own image in their neighbors.

---

*. My son. (Tr.)

†. Ominous. (Tr.)

‡. Persecution, atrocity. (Tr.)

Young women and new brides were repulsed by their fiancés and husbands and pushed them away. They had adored them when, in the most ecstatic days of rage and fury, eyes bloodshot, chins raised, belts cinched, they had snatched their guns and headed toward martyrdom for the holy struggle.

Foreign imams from distant lands had ridden through the village, waving their green flags, and howling the startling alarm, "Islam is under threat!... the *giaours** have risen up!..."

And so, those of military age had assembled, panting impatiently, and, for fear of falling behind, they had even refused the final embraces of their loved ones.

"Never mind your livestock and women!... what belongs to the *giaour* is bound to be yours sooner or later."

And they had still adored them when they returned from battle, when, covered in blood and weighed down with spoils, they nestled into the shelter of their hearths and declared that where they had been, not even an ear of corn was left standing and alive.

That was how the Muslim lands that stretched all the way to the surrounding mountains and well beyond them had been purged of that filthy populace.

"We'd enter the villages from the east and leave from the west, and whenever we'd look back, we'd see that everything was leveled to the ground. That's how it was wherever we went."

Girls danced for their heroes, and as they moved, rows of bracelets snatched from the arms of *giaours* jangled on their dusky forearms.

But now the peasant women, invisible behind their thick veils, followed their men's misery and terror with pitiless and indifferent eyes, as though somehow their destinies had parted ways. Only the crones wept incessantly, crying their oooh's of lament like a bunch of owls.

"*Amaaan!*†..." they moaned as they huddled outside their cottages, "what goes around comes around..."

---

*. Infidel. (Tr.)

†. A cry of lament. (Tr.)

And because deep down they felt that they had been ignorant, and, hence, blameless, both young and old, man and woman, obstinately sought those who were truly responsible.

"May the people behind all this be cursed! We used to live in peace and quiet; they drove us into this hell, whoever they are!..."

And they sometimes expressed compassion for the victims.

"I weep for them. We were like brothers. We used to eat from the same plate, drink from the same jug. How did they manage to turn them against us and us against them?... I grieve for the lives they lost. They died too soon!..."

Every day, more devastating news arrived from the surrounding Muslim villages and stirred the anxieties of Charpunar's villagers. Policemen and gendarmes on horseback continued their hunt for Habib and would almost always arrive after his departure. They would arrest anyone who had taken him in and search their homes. If they discovered any loot, they would take their owners away in chains.

Mothers and children mourned, their joy crushed, their daily bread poisoned... what kind of evil was assailing them?

"May Allah have mercy..." muttered the elderly as they stood trembling over their canes, "what else can we do!..."

Eventually Charpunar's villagers began to hope that they would find and capture Habib, as though sacrificing him could relieve the village of its nightmarish terror. They started accusing him of being the most ruthless of them all and almost deserving of the punishment meted out to him!...

"His sword had no pity, no mercy. Not for the mothers, not for the elderly. It even struck down babies at their mother's breast. They died a slow and painful death... Like a demon he was, like a scourge from hell..."

The villagers' sentiments even extended to Habib's brothers. And that is why whenever his mother would beseech her sons to go and find the fugitive and offer him every available means of protection, they would refuse and say, "What made him think he had the right to kill that way, in cold blood! He must pay for what he did... We killed too, but no one's coming for us. His hands took bodies that were already broken and chopped them into bits... He made us sick, and we walked away in disgust... He would pull the guts out of children that were still alive... He played around with their blood and their pain! The *devlet** got wind of what he did. Even they were sick with horror. He has no one to blame but himself! And now he can try to save his own neck for all we care ..."

Every night, all three brothers, wordless, grave, and ashen, would sit kneeling on the floor for hours on end, while their mother would sob inconsolably. Sleep had forsaken their eyes. Before them flickered the wan lamplight ...

When they finally went up to the roof to rest, they saw many other villagers, unable to sleep, their ghostly silhouettes visible across rooftops near and far.

***

"In the name of Allah, I swear to you!... if I find out where he is, I'll take him myself and turn him in to the *devlet*!..."

The gaunt black face of Habib's brother assumed the outlines of an indescribable grimace. His small, sharp, and restless eyes averted his mother's gaze...

With the ferocity of a tigress, the old woman stood up to her son, and her yellowed broken teeth seemed ready to shoot out of her gums.

"What a waste, the milk I fed you!... you're a bastard to me and a bastard to your brother! Say that again! Say it if you dare!"

"Oh yes, I'll hand him in," he repeated a little more softly and shut up.

His mother wanted to reply, but her rage drowned in her tears. She knelt on the ground and started to sob as she covered her eyes with a corner of her veil.

"Habib, *oghloom*, it's not just you that I lost. I don't have any sons left!... Your own home is now your enemy, and your brothers want you dead!... Come back and see what happened to all those friends of yours who fought at your side... I wish I had a martyr for a son; those mothers are lucky! They don't have to weep like I do!..."

---

*. State. (Tr.)

By and by, Habib's brother softened, eyes brimming with tears. He blinked and looked around, sighing at times at his mother's words. Eventually, he bent low, knelt before his mother, and tried to explain.

"*Anneh*,* you're in a lot of pain, but you're not alone, have a look around!... Look at what's happened to us! There's a curse on this village, it's doomed by some kind of evil... The wise men, the fortunetellers are saying that we're being punished for Habib's crimes, because he got out of hand, went on a rampage... *Anneh!*... If you saw him that day, you wouldn't recognize him... He was like a demon, a monster. Even his sword resisted. So, Habib used his fingers to tear them apart; he went after children and helpless women..."

The old woman shed her tears softly, without a word, but she said all at once, "A curse on the people who heaped all this on our heads. It wasn't your fault! I hope they drop dead, and their bones never rest in peace. Where are they now, those men who roused you to your feet? They pulled the wool over your eyes and got the better of you! Why didn't you listen to your father? You went against Islam, and this is your punishment for it."

Deep in bitter and black thoughts, their faith shaken, dispirited, mother and son kept their peace for a long while as they reflected on the immeasurable misery afflicting the village.

Indeed, the village of Charpunar was descending deeper into despair. New misfortunes piled up every day on top of everything that had already transpired. Disoriented and petrified, the villagers had neglected all their tasks. Spurred by hunger, their cattle wandered to nearby pastures and grazed on the sparse slips of straw jutting out of the rocky soil. The ashes from smoldering wine presses and cotton fields that had once belonged to Armenians blew in on the southerly wind, withering even the meadows along the riverbank. The brooks and springs had dried up and the well-water stank of decomposing bodies.

Diseases that were once unknown to the villagers suddenly cropped up overnight among the livestock; countless animals dropped dead in their pens as though a scythe had struck them down one by one. Some of the horses had broken out of their stables and run away like mad, as

---

*. Mother. (Tr.)

though their own manes were flogging them to charge ahead, their eyes glazed over, their nostrils flaring, invincible like dragons. Those that had stayed behind in the village wasted away from incurable diseases, their ribs hollowed out, their spines shriveled, their eyes fading deeper into their sockets and their incessant nightly pain-stricken neighing disturbed the villagers' already disrupted and troubled sleep.

The dogs guarding the village began to foam at the mouth, attacking their masters and their flocks of sheep like a pack of wolves. They howled as they chewed on their own limbs, leaving bloodstains in their tracks.

And then sometimes, suddenly, as though a collective terror had taken hold of them, they would start to yelp in unison, releasing long, ominous, and horrifying squeals. And people would sit up all at once in their cottages or on the mats spread out over the rooftops. Tossing and turning like the tormented souls of hell, they dreaded to think of what new evil was making itself known.

Equal to the Crime, the Punishment proved to be merciless, inveterate, unyielding. And that is why as the villagers began to recall their actions, they were consumed with terror. And just as the thirsty yearn for water, they yearned for the peace of death, because they suspected that resistance against such fateful damnation was futile, futile.

The old sage women had already recited their mysterious folk prayers and incantations over those that were struck by misfortune. They had been the first to witness that the evil would not disperse. Talismans brought from distant holy lands, prescriptions imbued with the spirits of dervishes, which were usually all-powerful and all-healing, proved to be entirely ineffective. There was no way out now, nothing left to be done. And after wrestling with the evil for some time, the village had given in and withdrawn into its ill-fated shell.

***

After a day of sweltering heat, the onset of evening brought some unexpectedly cool air. The relentless scorching sun had shone all day, blinding everyone and parching all the vegetation. It even seemed to dry the blood that was still pulsing through some beings' veins. The leaves on the trees turned yellow and crumbled into dust before falling to the

ground. Even the grains of sand were emanating the light and heat that
they had absorbed from the sun.

Their tongues parched, their mouths pasty, their eyes glazed over,
the villagers of Charpunar charged out of their homes and cottages when
the sun disappeared over the horizon. In this season, the heat was intense
every year. But this year, it seemed as though the impassive world of
inanimate objects along with nature's various elements had assumed a
different aspect. Not even the elderly could recall a time from their
distant past when it had been this hellish, when the water had
completely dried up. All that was left were the wells, where, in previous
years, they had been able to retrieve some water. But this year!... ooph....
ooph... So, they were destined to burn in the very fires that they had set.
So, their children and mothers were destined to be struck down by the
very same blows that they had struck...

In their thoughtless demented frenzy, they had awakened Death and
whetted its appetite... From the four corners of the horizon, as far as the
eye could see, not a single Armenian village remained. The enemy *millet**
had been destroyed over many hours... and then over many days...

Death had befriended them. It walked alongside them, invisible and
malevolent, and it had abided by their violent attacks... But when they
had returned to their village, weary and sated, death had not let them go.
It had clung on to their every step, and it slithered behind them into the
village, sheltering beneath their own roofs.

They had awakened death and whetted its appetite, and it was as
insatiable as a hyena.

It was that night that old Khoorshid, one of the most respected
women in the village, came forward and declared that she believed there
was a well which had not been contaminated. Instantly, all the women,
old and young, swung their clay jugs over their shoulders and assembled
to form a procession. The men, almost all fugitives, regarded the women
dubiously. They too knew that well, but until that day, and despite the
scarcity of water, they had not dared mention it, because getting there
meant they had to pass by the mountain, where Armenian villages lay

---

*. A semi-autonomous confessional community – notably, non-Muslim –
in the Ottoman Empire. (Tr.)

scattered in ruins. Weeks had passed since those murderous days, and still none of them had returned to the heaps of ashes. Even when they needed to pass by the Armenian villages on their way to nearby fields or to other Muslims villages, they chose to lengthen their trip by making a detour at the furthest possible point. They shuddered at seeing any sign or semblance of the crime committed at their hands. And they bristled especially at the thought that they might run into widows or orphans who might have returned to their hearths.

But their thirst was intense. An inferno scorched their throats and bowels… And they let the women go and retrieve some clean water for the village.

Hours went by. The star-studded firmament was tinted with a deep violet hue. There was no moon, yet a pale white light filtering through a pearly fog cast its glow all around. Undulations of peaks and valleys. Occasionally, the southerly wind blew waves of warm air, carrying the odor of dry charred earth tinged with the nauseating whiff of rotting corpses.

The women hurried as they hunched beneath the weight of their brimming jugs. They said nothing and listened to each other's strained breathing. Suddenly, old Khoorshid stopped, and the rest followed. She was shaking her head and pulling on her veil, so that they would not see the expression on her face. Because she could feel it contort, despite her best efforts. But her resolve swiftly crumpled; she dropped her veil, and started to screech, "I knew about all of it!… But I didn't try to stop them… Now there's nothing but ruins for the orphans and widows!…"

She pointed at the misty mountains and repeated in horror, "There's nothing but pain beyond that peak!…"

Everyone's gaze turned toward that line on the horizon and something extraordinary ensued… Those days seemed to return… The stars in the sky faded into a burning crimson and as though the gates of hell had been unleashed, the clouds burst into flames that loomed all the way to the farthest reaches of the horizon… Screaming and wailing!… They were haunted by the vision of unburied bodies whose decaying scattered bones reassembled and stood up before their astonished eyes… Right beside them, they could hear the dying as they drew their final breaths... The stones and earth seemed to be speaking, and they heard voices emanating from every crevice...

Raving and terrified, the young women closed their ears and screamed as though they were being struck by a barrage of relentless blows. In their disgust, some discarded the water, which vanished instantly into the desiccated earth and flames. Some of them even smashed their jugs into the ground.

Old Khoorshid continued to scream, "There's nothing but pain beyond that peak!..."

Her dark emaciated body quaked, her chin trembled, but her finger kept pointing at the same spot.

In the white glow of the twinkling stars, an elusive black silhouette slithered along the foothills across the way. Perhaps it could hear the women's shrieks. Its palms pressed to the ground, it raised its head and looked around. The women saw it move, and it seemed to them that the mountain, baked hard with the blood of its children, shook loose from its foundations and threatened them with vengeance.

Their jugs scattered across the ground, their veils in tatters, they fled every which way, and, in their delirium, they wandered off the road, heading further away from the village as their bare feet bled on the white craggy ground. Sometimes they fell down face first, tripping with every step, as though countless specters, persistent and untiring, were taking turns to tug at their shoulders...

Slithering along the ground like a snake and needlessly terrified, the fugitive's black shadow appeared and disappeared among the twinkling white stars. It was Habib... They were all born in the same village, some of them had been his playmates, they had grown up together, but they did not recognize each other. They fled as though they were running from a ruthless unsparing enemy.

***

When the sun rose and scattered its fiery rays over the deserted pastures and barren fields, the most elderly of Charpunar's villagers, old men hunched over their canes, dragged their atrophied, paralyzed limbs through the road's chalky dust, and left the village. Following behind them were those who were left in the dark by their untimely blindness, their faces upturned toward the searing sky, their arms outstretched, groping the backs of their elderly companions so as not to deviate from the path. A bitter yearning disturbed the peace on these old people's faces, and they said nothing, so as not to hear the ominous significance of the words that might escape their lips.

That is what the villagers had decided. A few days earlier, they had learned that Sheikh Ali, the renowned medium, was going to pass through their village. Despite the entreaties of the men that they had dispatched to Sheikh Ali, the old man did not want to step foot onto the land of a murderous village… No, no!... They had transgressed against laws both Human and Divine. He sensed that the evil done at their hands was irremediable. They had drawn the tears of mothers and children, those idiots! He was going to strangle them. Allah the Just would exact His revenge for many a century, and His temper is unyielding… And unquestionable!...

"Only the elderly, blind, and infirm," the Sheikh had pronounced, "those who did not leave their homes. I'm willing to meet with only the blind and the infirm, at the rest-stop, beneath the shade of a mulberry tree."

The old men had been walking for some time. Sweat poured down from the white caps on their heads. Their feeble legs buckled, and the dry tapping of their canes anticipated their echoing steps.

Merciless and searing, the sun beat down on the napes of their wrinkled necks and the bare soles of their feet blistered on the rocky ground.

Sometimes, the southerly wind passed over them like a crashing wave. But rather than offering some relief, it made them grimace, because it was saturated with the stench of corpses that had been left to rot.

And sometimes, foul hideous swarms of beetles and flies would halt their creeping, wobbling flight along the ground and suddenly rise, shrouding them like a black mist. Their elderly hands tried in vain to shoo away those ominous little creatures. But their gluey, hairy feet stuck to their skin, crept into the corners of their eyes and the rims of their nostrils, as their appetites were stirred by the stench of death wafting through the air.

And so, the elderly men of Chapunar walked on, through this excruciating ordeal, until they finally reached the designated location, far from the accursed village, where they hoped to be enlightened about their terrible misfortunes.

***

At one time, pious and virtuous hands had planted mulberry trees along this desolate and treeless road, so that parched travelers could sate themselves with their fruits and have a moment's rest in the cover of their lush, generous canopies. Over the years, they had multiplied and gained in strength, and their shadow extended across a wide area. The elderly had gazed upon those trees and taken comfort in them since their childhood. Many village dwellers from the region, both Armenian and Muslim, had rested in their shade. During the cotton harvest, when the women and girls would leave their villages to work the fields for a few weeks, they would unroll their mats in that spot at night. And the cradles of nursing babies would dangle from their freshest, most pliable boughs, as they had for several generations.

This time, across the desolate and bare expanse of fields, the trees did not appear to the old men's bleary searching eyes. Because on their return from killing and pillaging, the vile murderers had viciously felled them with their bloody axes. And, their stout branches lay scattered near their beheaded trunks, like the remains of human skeletons.

Pious and virtuous people had planted them for the benefit of travelers and, after eliminating an entire living generation, the intransigent enemy had tried to eliminate even their forebears' good intentions... shady canopies for thirsty travelers...

Now a scraggy black-and-white horse, blanketed in dry leaves, was searching for those robust shady trees. Because after the formation of the Military Tribunal, the constant traffic prompted officers, policemen and other employees to build a rest-stop along the road. That was where the caravans of constantly relocated prisoners and convicts – as well as those wandering Armenians who were put in chains after their miraculous survival – were also made to stop.

***

In that terrible heat, the *kahveji*,[*] a tall slender Circassian, rolled out some straw mats, where the group of old men sat cross-legged after setting aside their canes. Just then, as though they were seeing each other for the very first time, they exchanged heartbroken and tearful greetings.

"*Aleykum selam!...*"[†]

"*Selam aleykum!...*"[‡]

Their calloused hands rose to their breasts, and they bowed their heads to humbly accept the greetings. But uncertainty returned to their eyes, and their lips became mute. Occasionally, a heartbroken sigh rose from one of their breasts.

"Ooph...Oph!"

The Circassian huddled on the ground, blowing into a fire lit from cotton brush to start preparing the *kahveh* and to kindle the coals for the nargilehs. Sometimes, the smoke would stifle his breath, and he would walk away from his work, take a seat, and raise his head simply to observe the old men.

They kept their peace, until one of the blind men broke the silence, "May Allah grant us His infinite mercy... Our brave sons did wrong and are paying the price..."

"That's true, that's true, they did wrong and are paying the price..."

The Circassian prepared the *kahveh* and approached barefoot to serve the old men. He then brought the nargilehs and placed one by each man, tucking the pipes into the blind ones' arthritic hands.

"Evil...evil..." cried another. "Doom is nesting in our homes, brothers are turning on brothers, sisters are spiting their sisters – our fields are barren, our cattle destroyed, our flocks butchered... A cruel, invisible hand is crushing our lives. Women are suddenly dropping dead, some have lost their minds, and miscarriages are striking those with child. Many have been raving in broad daylight as though they are possessed... Everywhere we turn, there is nothing but terror and

---

*. Coffee vendor. (Tr.)

†. Peace be upon you. (Tr.)

‡. And upon you, peace. (Tr.)

suspicion. We're like dry leaves being tossed around by an evil wind... Eyes have lost their light; smiles have faded from children's lips. Our village's best men are no better now than ferocious animals, wild and furious... What is this thing, this invisible, never-ending disaster that is hanging over us?..."

"A curse!... a curse!..."

***

The Sheikh had arrived and was standing beside them, but the old men were distracted. And they could hear the pronouncement reverberate in all four corners of the horizon, from the great expanse of fields to the distant blue foothills: a curse!... a curse!... And now they seemed puzzled, unable to tell whether that voice was rising within them or reaching their ears from beyond.

The Sheikh had been standing beside them, and when their perplexed faces turned toward him, no one was able to conceive that his pursed, pale lips may have been the ones that spoke those ominous words.

The Sheikh was a confounding man. He was both respected and scorned. He made daily visits to the villages to receive, with head held high, the meager alms so vital for his existence. But occasionally, he would disappear for a time. And when he returned, they would notice that he appeared to be darker, more wrinkled. When the harvests were good, the livestock healthy, the springs and brooks babbling, who would have given any credence to his supposed supernatural powers? They dismissed him entirely when he was of no use. And the Sheikh would resign himself to his role as a common, proverbial itinerant beggar.

But, when times took a turn for the worse, he would instantly acquire all that he had ever wished for and all the influence in the world. Then, the superstitious, anxious villagers would ache for his visit, approaching him with the reverence and supplication that were usually reserved for saints... When times took a turn for the worse!... the Sheikh would assume a different form. The small black eyes set in that face of a thousand wrinkles would shoot out a bluish flame, and he would turn deathly pale. His colorless, frail limbs would tighten and tense, and he would become a prophet, pontificating with exhortations and admonishments. And even men of great standing would bow their heads before him, although his claims almost always contradicted majority opinion, sentiment, and temperament. It was as though the Sheikh employed supernatural powers to momentarily open the illuminated horizons of equanimity and wisdom among those stubborn, ignorant, dim, and primitive minds. But when the evil was vanquished and the villagers returned their thoughts to their lands, they would forget all about the Sheikh, his exhortations, and warnings amid their minor day-to-day tasks. That is when, silent, spiteful, and alone, he would resume his perambulations through the villages, enduring the life of an ascetic and mendicant dervish.

The Sheikh sat down at a slight remove from the group of old men and remained still. He just shook his head occasionally, as announced by the rocking of his conical white calpac. His features had assumed an unusual pallor resembling the whitish grey of embers that had long been extinguished. When he would quietly open his eyelids, his glassy white eyes, where his pupils seemed to slip out of sight, would elicit a sudden fright. Those eyes' uncommon expression indicated that this man chosen by God could communicate through supernatural powers.

In the pervading fearful silence, one of the old blind men of Charpunar finally spoke up, hoarse and dejected, "Brother, may you be kind and merciful to our children… our misery could not get any worse… even our enemies now have pity on us."

They all broke down in tears, and as they suddenly realized the infinite pathos in his words, all the old men repeated in a single raspy, ragged voice, "Even our enemies now have pity on us."

At first, the Sheikh kept quiet. Stretching his whole body forward, he bowed, and his limbs looked as though they were about to snap like dry stooping branches. A cold sweat beaded on his cadaverous face and instead of words, bubbles of frothing spit rose to his lips.

The old men were sobbing quietly. Every tear streamed painfully from their ailing and bleary eyes. After a moment's pause, the blind man asked, "Brother, may you be kind and merciful to our children and our innocent grandchildren. Please tell us, what is the nature of the evil that has struck us and what is its source?"

The Sheikh shifted and yelled, "A curse!... a curse!..."

For the old men, heaven and earth went black once more and, once more, after echoing a thousandfold among the mountains and valleys, the Sheikh's cry returned to them, "A curse, a curse!..."

The vault of heaven above them, the sun and all of nature's colors and forms, the countless particles of earth beneath their feet, and even the blood rushing through their own temples with a pulsating swish, everything, every feature, and every sound repeated the Sheikh's ominous cry, "A curse!... a curse!..."

So, even nature's elements had now become their enemies. The earth had not swept over the blood that had spilled from its truest children, and the punishment was going to be, now and forevermore, proportionate to the crime that was committed.

They themselves had not taken part in that crime, but they knew its horrific and shocking details all too well. And the more they recalled the innocent blood spilled at their children's hands, the more they quaked and shuddered at the thought of the punishment, because they knew that it would take more than several consecutive generations to expiate their guilt.

"What can we do," whimpered one of the other old men, "how can we soften the curse cast by the victims and all those who were wronged? Tell us, and we will pay for our grandchildren's happy futures with our own pale blood."

The Sheikh was skeptical and shook his head. He turned his gaze to each of them and, in his upraised eyes, he projected the cold hard image of irreparable misery. But after a moment's silence, he commanded the grieving old men who were listening with bated breath, "Return the loot to their rightful owners."

"They have all been killed."

"Well then, return them to their widows and orphaned children."

"We don't know where they have gone. They keep running from us in fright and many of them burned to death in their homes."

"Take back their belongings, I tell you, and keep nothing for yourselves. Throw them into their graves."

"They don't have any graves, oh Sheikh… They burnt to ashes in the fires or were left unburied and unclaimed… Their hacked bodies were thrown into the wells and the river, and those that were left out in the sun were torn apart by scavenging animals."

They had not finished speaking when the Sheikh stood, picked up his sandals, turned his back on the old men of Charpunar, and walked away.

They saw him for a long while on the long white road. He never turned to look at them. Sometimes, they thought they noticed the gentle rocking of the Sheikh's conical calpac. And they assumed that in his solitary outrage, he kept repeating his commands, all along the long white road.

***

"Tears shed by widows and orphans are the deadliest venom … Woe to those who draw those tears."

"Woe to those who draw those tears," repeated the old men softly and hopelessly.

A dry, broken cackle drew their attention. Right beside them, on the very same mat, there stood a creature that looked almost human. His matted, dusty hair caked his head like dry mortar, giving a vague roundness to the outline of his skull, as though it had been shaved. His deeply tanned, wind-ravaged face peered at them with the eyes of a beast. His tattered clothes hung in pieces off his limbs. Nettles had scratched his thin sinewy forearms, and every conceivable type of insect bite had raised sores all over his chest and arms… One could no longer discern either his age or his class and would be hard pressed to find any mark of humanity in his features. But the old men instantly recognized him. It was Habib… His suntanned skin was so opaque that the blood seemed to have evaporated from his face, and his cadaverous complexion made him look terrifying. He held a fresh sprig of poplar, and he waved it around as he cackled with mouth agape, while his eyes fixed on an obscure point in the distance.

When had he come to join them? They had no idea. When they were listening to the Sheikh, he too had heard those commands and had noted, perhaps for the very first time, the black letters etched into his forehead.

What was written could not be unwritten... And from the day he had slipped free of his mother's womb, he had been heading in that direction... toward the gallows... In that obscure distance which held fast his gaze, he finally saw that torture device where his body had been hanged... The old men's eyes followed his gaze, and even the blind ones turned their brows. They could all see that, hanging among the numerous gallows, swung the body of the village head's son, Habib...

The condemned man shuddered with indescribable terror. And he tried to move his eyes away from that point but failed. He shuddered once more and then seemed to come to his senses. He managed to turn his head away. For a moment, no one spoke. But, little by little, Habib became more agitated and started to tear off the poplar sprig's leaves. Suddenly and unexpectedly, he said, "They hanged three more Muslims this morning."

He cackled all the while like a madman. At times, he could have been the village idiot, the consummate image of an oblivious dimwit, but his eyes... As though they had broken free of his dark soul, they existed in a terror all their own... The old men gazed upon those eyes, which seemed to behold with magnified and uninterrupted clarity all that had transpired in those ill-fated days, while they also saw what was about to unfold....

And they were all increasingly convinced that if that one could be sacrificed, Charpunar could perhaps be saved from the curse. They turned to each other, and as if reading each other's thoughts, they signaled to the eldest among them to take the floor.

In his most persuasive voice, "Habib, *oghloom*," he said, "come sit with us and hear what we have to say..."

Yielding to the old man's coaxing tone, he fell to his knees and stayed rooted to his spot...

"Hear what those of us at the brink of death have to say... Do you think you can keep running this way? Do you think you can hide?... Didn't you hear the Sheikh? There's no point fighting it... What is written cannot be unwritten... Wouldn't it better to simply accept your fate?... Have some dignity, redeem yourself, and then depart from this passing empty world…"

Habib was no longer laughing and watched them gravely. He opened his mouth several times to speak, but his jaws moved in vain. He then shouted clearly for all to hear, "I am not afraid of death!..."

But what a strange alien voice that was. His own ears could not recognize those words as they left his lips.

"I am not afraid of death!..."

Habib had uttered those words frequently, honestly, and with great faith. He had pronounced them before the events and even as he had headed off to fight. He remembered that, before the crimes were committed, that voice had been his own… But back then, he did not know death, did not understand it, and he marched brashly towards it.

He had first seen death in his own hands, on his own victims… He had seen it in the gleaming startled eyes of children as they went dark as the midday sun went black over this land… He had seen it in mothers' eyes as they shut at the sight of their children's blood… He had heard it in the heartrending, desperate shrieks, entreaties, struggles… He had felt it in the tremors of torn tendons, had touched it when the warm blood that had spilled into his hands had eventually cooled… Death!... That is what death meant to him – twitching limbs, twisted faces, horrified eyes, and gagged syllables on blanching lips, and sobbing, groaning, choking… That is what death meant to him, horrific, revolting – death, tormenting and terrifying – death, of beings full of life and vigor – death, murderous – death, untimely…

And this thing called death meant many things to him, as it multiplied according to the number of his crimes. Because as he breathed his last, he would do so with the agony of all those who breathed their last when they were murdered by his hand – he would die their excruciating deaths.

And now, Habib was terrified of that death. He dreaded it, fled from it, he feared it in soul, he feared it in body, and every fiber of his being shuddered from that death and shunned it…

To become the world's most terrible being, but to live, to live, to live!... To crawl on one's belly, to be a reptile living among ruins and crevices, to be a desiccated bush, to turn to stone, to be piled up among the rocks!... To be the downtrodden earth, but to live, to live, to live!...

And in his infinite and unbearable weakness, Habib pleaded for his life to the old men, his *hemsherries*,[*] who remained icy, blind. He pleaded to lifeless objects, to the sun, the sky, the air, and the flocks of black birds flying in the distance. He even begged the beetles and the worms squirming underground. But they all, all of them faded away, vanished, and his world became a void, darkening in the face of his terror.

The old man continued to speak, but Habib was no longer listening, no longer hearing him...

"The blood that you spilled is going to drown us... Every drop demands its price... They were innocent, they were our neighbors. We broke bread together... Habib, *oghloom*, accept your punishment, redeem yourself, and then depart from this passing empty world..."

At that point, the Circassian came and stood before them, announcing that he could hear horses' hooves in the distance. Habib sprang up and slipped away from the old men who began stammering in their confusion as they considered the situation and muttered some half-spoken commands in their alarm. Then, several of them lay down and pressed their ears to the ground, listening for the riders' location and speed. They could hear the steady rhythm of horses' hooves underground, as though a heart throbbing down below wanted to rouse the earth out of its vast indifference.

The riders finally appeared on the horizon. They were approaching fast, and now their uniforms' buttons and trims could be seen, glittering as they came within range of the old men's line of sight. The Circassian, shielding his eyes from the sun with his hand, looked up and recognized them.

"Policemen!... gendarmes!..."

"Brothers of the same blood and the same race."

To which the Circassian seemed to respond with his timid reply, "The policemen of *hoorriyet*[†]..."

---

[*]. Fellow countrymen. (Tr.)

[†]. Liberty. (Tr.)

***

Darkness had enclosed the land and for several hours, perfect silence reigned all around. Black thunderclouds rolled through the sky and passed without rainfall. Despite the cloud cover, the daytime heat was even more stifling. Waves of reeking winds rolled in from all directions, wafted and then receded. Strange unidentifiable flies and mosquitoes that were at the ready to bite attacked people's bare limbs, and children were covered with small blistery sores... As the air grew heavy from the approaching storms, flashes of lightening sometimes seemed to tear through the sky, and sometimes it would thunder but not rain, while the clouds – black, threatening, and tempestuous – loomed as far as the eye could see across the heavens of Cilicia.

Darkness had enclosed the whole world, and one could no longer see the line dividing land and sky. Villages and hamlets were as still and gloomy as graveyards. And Habib was as elusive as a shadow while he wandered through that night. He had gone into hiding as soon as he had seen the policemen on the thoroughfare. He ran at a frantic and senseless pace, without pause, without rest, terrified by his own shadow and even startled by the slightest noise of the evening wind creeping through the sands beneath his feet. He was suspicious of even the most secret hideouts, of which only he knew. And he could not entrust his body either to the foothills or to the ruins of ancient fortresses. But he was now exhausted and hungry, as though an unquenchable raging fire blazed in his parched breast and bowels, and his head pounded as though it had come under a hammer's rapid blows.

Eventually, in his mad aimless flight, he neared his natal village and began to circle closer to it.

One night's rest in his mother's home!... Just one night. He felt straightaway the sweet tranquility of his native threshold, their oxen's musky breath, the scent of straw, and the clay jug's cool touch on his thirsty lips...

"The pomegranate trees must have blossomed," he thought all at once...

And their beautifully fiery flowers danced in his mind like tiny flames.

Darkness had enclosed land and sky. There was no sound, not even a whisper. Like all the other villages along his way, Charpunar was as still as a graveyard… as though all the homes and hamlets had been abandoned. That is when Habib slunk into the village like a thief.

The village head's sons were asleep, weary from the oppressive heat. But their mother was keeping watch… She watched the threatening sky, and her anxious, tormented thoughts wandered to the fate of her youngest son. Night and day, she awaited news from the birds, the winds, and the clouds passing overhead. Sometimes, the old women strove to console her, but she would shake her head and mumble, "I would not wish a mother's anguish on a cur…"

When Habib reached his home, his loud panting alerted his mother to his presence. Stepping softly, she climbed down from the roof and led her fugitive son to a room on the first floor, where they usually stored the wheat. The room was now bare, and only a pile of straw lay in one corner. Mother and son dragged the straw toward them in the dark, spread them across the floor and sat down. Habib was still panting, drool pouring from his gaping mouth. His mother quickly tended to her son, with no need for questions as she gleaned his most pressing needs by intuition and habit. When the jug reached Habib's lips, he drank in one breathless gulp, his eyes rolling back as though he was about to faint.

"Habib, *oghloom*," his mother sobbed uncontrollably and could say no more.

"*Anneh*," Habib said finally… "they're after me, they're looking for me, I heard on my way back that I was condemned to death and didn't come home. I was so hungry and thirsty, *anneh*, and the stones and the mountains, none of them had any pity on me."

His eyes rolled back once more… He was dizzy. In the darkness, even darker shapes moved at extraordinary speeds across his eyes.

Mother and son had forgotten the rest of the world. Their own personal misfortunes were all that appeared before their eyes, and they did not for an instant take heed of the roots of those misfortunes, of the crimes that had been committed, and of all the other mothers who were left to mourn.

"*Anneh*, keep me here tonight," stammered Habib, "and I'll leave before daybreak so no one will know I was here."

It was already midnight, and Habib was sleeping soundly on the scattered straw. His mother went up to the roof to avoid raising her other sons' suspicions.

***

Habib had been asleep for two hours when he awoke all at once as though he had been roused. He thought it was his mother, and his heavy, bitter-tasting tongue was barely able to utter, "It's still early, *anneh*... the cock hasn't crowed yet..." As if to respond, at that very instant the cock let out its shrill, clear, and lingering voice...

Habib sat up on his mat and listened. A moment of total silence followed and then, more cocks took their turns to crow across other parts of the village.

It was still dark and not a single ray of light had seeped into the room. He believed, however, that the time had come for him to depart.

Lack of sleep had made him delirious. His thigh was weak and maimed, his feet bleeding, and all his limbs throbbed with various aches and pains. The air was noticeably fresher, and the sweat on his back felt cool. With his eyes staring into the dark, he began to think, "I won't be able to see the village in daylight... I have to leave... I feel like I'm blind... The pomegranate trees must have blossomed, but I won't be able to see them... and I won't have my share of their fruits... *Anneh*... *Anneh*... *Anneh!*..."

He sang his sorrows quietly to himself, and even the most trivial details in his memories became larger than life. He craved to see, he craved to hear, he craved to smell and eat everything that, since childhood, he had seen, heard, and fed on. His senses ached, piercing him with their various longings, and he thirsted for the familiar shapes and colors of that life. Suddenly, everything jumbled in his mind, a powerful vertigo paralyzed him, and a series of hallucinations struck his eyes and ears.

Voices!... voices!... voices... The horse-mounted gendarmes and officers were approaching at a galloping pace!... So, the villagers were awake?... What's that noise? A mob!... Are they howling or weeping?... *Anneh!... anneh!... anneh...*

In an instant, the room was teeming with a great multitude. They were putting him in chains and taking him away, but he resisted! They pulled at him, and his limbs began to bleed as they were dragged along the ground. And that was how they were taking him away, leaving trails of blood in their wake...

"I don't want to die!... *anneh!* I'm terrified of dying!... Hide me, cover me!... *Anneh*, they're going to hang me!..."

A white light appeared in the sky. The earth was still dark. But the rooftops and the mountaintops in the distance were becoming paler. A voice whispered in his ear, "What is written cannot be unwritten." But he refused to hear that unseemly voice and thought with terror that it was the hour of his execution, the time set at the break of day.

And so, he finally saw that nightmarish device, and it was far taller than it had seemed, rooted much more firmly into his native soil.

Where were his comrades in arms at that moment, the Muslim villagers, the imams who had incited them to massacre and loot?... Where were they?... People had eyes but could not see, they had ears but could not hear... What was that hostile mob that was churning like the sea?... enemies who wanted to take his life.

Bitter, gloomy hopelessness enclosed his soul, and he no longer screamed or pleaded or hoped. Light as a feather, they placed him at the foot of the gibbet. It was there, standing before him... not another sound, not another whisper. People were moving about like shadows, working in perfect silence... He too seemed to be losing his solidity... but he was still there... standing before the gallows...

The dawn light became paler over the rooftops and the distant mountains. He turned around and now there was no one left!... They had all fled, escaped! He was alone, standing before the gallows, and his solitary shadow stretched alongside that of the gibbet in the pale morning light.

Suddenly, his shadow broke free from him, took on a form of its own and stood before him... Oh the horror, it was the executioner, unearthly, uncanny, a being from beyond!... It was the executioner, and it was his own likeness... He knew him as clearly as he knew his own reflection in the streams. He was as pale as a corpse, and his demented eyes were trained on him.

They stood there for a time, face to face, at the foot of the gallows. And, one moment, Habib was the executioner, while the next, he was the convict... The morning light became even paler, and the proceedings lagged, because they had forgotten the rope. Although it was light, the executioner had to rummage for it, hands fumbling as though he was blind. Habib watched and thought, "There was some rope in the corner of the storehouse and you didn't even know, you scoundrels!..."

But as soon as this thought occurred to him, the rope was found, and the executioner began to approach him with muted but unavoidable steps.

"Never!... never!..." Habib screamed, and he was panting, and he was resisting the executioner... This lasted for several long minutes... The cocks began to crow for the second time, and, like a distant spectator, Habib saw his neck slip through the noose and his hanging body sway from the gallows.

***

As soon as it got light, Habib's mother, anxious that Habib had not appeared, entered the storehouse to look for him, and in the light of the fresh sunrise, she saw her son's wretched body hanging from a beam on the ceiling.

The elderly mother cried and explained what had happened. But no one could understand what she was saying. She went knocking on doors, tearing out her hair, clawing at her face, begging for pity and condolences. As they watched her, men and women were at first stupefied by her words. But the terrible event finally penetrated the peasants' minds, "Habib killed himself! He hanged himself!..."

The old women took their places on their cottage thresholds and shook their heads in pain and confusion. Surprise mingled with horror in the fervently passionate eyes of young men, and at that moment, more and more of them felt crushed by the memories of their crimes. The blind and elderly were the last to hear the news, and through the tremors of their praying lips, they sometimes cried, "That's enough, Allah!... shine your mercy upon our never-ending sins, because the weight of the earth on the dead in their graves is not as heavy as the pain that crushes us now."

Meanwhile, in the black shadows of the storehouse, hanging from a dusty beam, Habib's body gently swayed.

It was not until around noon that the authorities learned of the event and sent policemen to remove his body.

They cut the rope, put his corpse on a stretcher and took it through the main thoroughfare. Everyone, women, men, and children lined both sides of the road and stood watching in the sun... They could all see Habib's monstrous blue face, his eyes bulging out of their sockets, his tongue black and stuck to his chin. There was not a single sound or whisper as they watched. And all the murderers thought that they were seeing themselves in that disfigured twisted corpse, because for just a few minutes, they lived through the same agony as those sentenced to death when they stand before the gallows.

***

The days and weeks passed. Some of Charpunar's villagers emigrated to distant lands, and some joined tribes of wandering nomads. Many homes were shuttered, and many a chimney no longer smoked. After the deadly drought, relentless torrential rains had turned even the ground in their homes into slippery silt. Not a palmful of dry soil remained. The river, savage and furious, had breached its banks and surged, carrying in its overwhelming currents everything that they had hidden in their underground pits... There was nothing left! And the currents had not only taken the victims' defiled belongings, but also all that the villagers had earned by the sweat of their brows.

The water seeped into everything, sometimes slithering underground and burrowing through the earth before erupting, striking at the foundations of homes and uprooting trees that were centuries old.

Even the cemeteries were in disarray. The village dead had been expelled from their graves and thrown back up to the surface. The water stirred their scattered bones according to its wicked whims.

For days on end, the river, furious and unforgiving, had roared past them. The fields, plains, and meadows had become lakes and reflected the threatening dark clouds overhead.

Old men and women, aware of their fate and resigned to it, would remind the young and bewildered, "*Haydan gelen huyda gider!...*"*

It seemed that heaven and earth, the mountains and rivers had revolted and were compensating for the lack of human justice. And when, without fail, the clouds continued to rumble and the flooded river continued to roar, it seemed to the villagers' disturbed imaginings that the vengeful spirit of the decimated race – undying and just, sublimely radiant – was soaring above their world and well beyond the limits set by their own ilk's disposition – that dark, violent force of evil.

---

*. Easy come, easy go. (Tr.)

Տիկ. Զ. ՆՍՍԱՅԵՆՆ
Ոշրուագիծ Ա․ Մուրատեանի

Safiyeh

That evening, as on every previous day, twilight cast a gloriously red glow. As the setting sun's radiant light fell over the foothills, it unfolded like muslin and glittered as far as the eye could see. The earth emerged through the peaks as crimson waves that tumbled onto the plains, but, at that hour, their usual harmony resounded with sobs.

Safiyeh had been waiting. For days and weeks, the bravest men of the village had congregated in whispers, and she was barely able to discern that the *giaours* were going to rebel, that the battle was nigh… Fighting had commenced that morning, and she knew that her son's arms, which were prepared to wage war for the glory and conquest of Allah, would be unshakeable and merciless. She had been the one to fasten his sword to his belt, and it was she who had loaded his gun. That morning, she had taken her son's horse by the reigns and led him to the edge of their village.

All the young men had left, and the old folk cursed their impotence, because they too were giddy with the intoxicating promise of blood. Meanwhile, the children tried to sneak away, as they felt too embarrassed to be stuck with the women, when their older brothers and fathers had left with sharpened blades and loaded guns.

The women and girls of the village had gathered on a plateau. Covering their faces with red *yazma*s,* they had watched all day as the battle unfolded in the surrounding villages… Their passionate eyes blazed beneath their dark *yazma*s, and they were quiet and still with the certainty of their men's victory.

All the *giaour* villages were in flames… They had spent all day tracking the mob as their hands shielded their eyes from the sun… The peaceful village on the distant line of the horizon had awakened in terror at dawn… Screams, shrieks… Many a human cry fell quiet when the wind was favorable, but then shooting, mayhem, chaos… The foreigners' gunshots gradually faded and stopped, while their men's guns, so familiar to their ears, continued to shoot without pause… Then

---

*. Traditional headscarf. (Tr.)

silence, and behind them, smoke rising from the burning village... All this went on until nightfall...

Their blades bloody and unsheathed, their shirts stained, their guns still smoking, the fighters returned in the evening, some together, others alone. They had brought back five Muslims who had been killed and a few wounded, and, while they were raging more than ever with hate, they were also dazzled by the riches of their loot.

Safiyeh continued to wait. At first, she had resigned herself to her fate. But her uneasy impatience made her wait harder to bear. Her hand on her cheek, her brows knitted, and her heart stout as a boulder, she looked for her son as she removed the shroud covering the face of each Muslim martyr who was brought back from the battlefield, while their widows and orphaned children let out long, mournful wails. Oooooh...oooh...

Twilight's golden rays began to dim over the mountains... The beautiful summits that she held so dear jutted upward, toward the overcast sky... They were blue at first, then violet, and finally black.

The sobs of the earth grew louder as a tide of corpses burdened its mountainous swells and obstructed their advance.

The voices in distant villages had died down, and the evening breeze blew blindly towards her, carrying the acrid smell of smoke from smoldering lands combined with the fumes of immolated bodies and stagnating blood... The remnants of farms, dwellings, and ploughs continued to smolder, and sometimes a splinter would suddenly ignite into a new blaze in the middle of the night... Heavy black clouds looming overhead jostled each other. They were joined by plumes of smoke and fire rising from the earth, which deepened the gloom in the celestial dome...

Safiyeh eventually turned her eyes away from this ominous scene and returned to her hut. No one on horseback entered her line of sight... A funereal silence reigned all around, disturbed occasionally by the breathy barks of instinctively fearful dogs and the mournful wails of Muslim widows.

"Ooooh...ooohh....oohhh..."

Old age had bent her low, and her eyes had become too dim for the joys of this world... Hardened by a trying, tough life, which often left her hungry, she was not susceptible to the emotional outbursts of women nor to passive sentimentality...

Her emotions were cruelly, cuttingly sharp... Persecuted from a young age, she belonged to a line of peoples who felt the indignity of their wounded Islamic honor and the weight of the foreigner's yoke... They had arrived from distant lands. Her father and husband had died in battle. And those losses had rendered her birthplace oppressive, hateful, and alien to her. So, she had emigrated with her son to the more forgiving and hospitable lands of Asia Minor... As their only belongings, she had brought with them her husband's and father's daggers and gun – which in peacetime, her son took hunting, and, in hard times, to fight.

And then the *devlet* had granted them their own land and even cultivable seeds. And after building a hut out of river reeds, they felt that they were no longer in want of the bare necessities... Old Safiyeh was even thinking of her son's marriage prospects, having already begun subjecting the village girls to her strict but impartial judgment, when alas, the fighting commenced...

Now she was waiting for her son. And, since, after the scorching day, there was a springtime chill in the evening air, she lit a fire with some cotton brush in anticipation of her son's return.

The hours passed. She knelt on the floor and blew into the fire to stoke the flames. The smoke blinded her, and her eyes watered. She wondered at times whether those tears welled up from an inner source.

Some kind neighbors returning from the fight had brought news of her son. They had seen him there well into the night. He had been braver than their bravest men. They had seen his eyes blaze with holy rage, his arms flexed, his shirt red with the blood of infidels. He had spared no one, neither men and boys nor women and the elderly. He fell upon the Armenian villages like a plague, a nightmare. He would tighten his belt, swiftly fasten his *yazma* to his fez, and then give the signal to attack.

"*Bismillah el Rahman ul Rahim...*"[*]

---

[*]. In the name of God, most Gracious, most Merciful. (Tr.)

The horses neighed, their nostrils flared, and their hooves trampled upon bloody human remains, upon bellies that were ripped open, and the tender bodies of butchered children...

He had been braver than their bravest men... That did not surprise her, but why hadn't he come home?...

Suddenly, her practiced ears heard a distant sound in the night... The fast rhythmic gallop of horses' hooves on the damp ground... Could it be?... The sound was approaching, entering the village, and after a moment, the horse came to a stop near the hut... It was her son... Relieved at last, she waited for him to tie the creature to the ancient mulberry tree and then welcomed him home.

The cotton brush fire crackled, and she was able to see her brave son in its light...

A deathly pallor had transformed his face. He had lost his fez, and his *yazma* fell crooked across his face... A tuft of black hair sprouting from his shaved head stuck to his sweaty forehead, and his legs were buckling, his arms trembling...

"Are you hurt?" asked his mother almost unconcerned.

"It's nothing, just a graze... There's no getting rid of that damned people!"

They were both quiet... At one point, her son wanted to speak, but his teeth began to chatter...

"You caught a cold, come closer to the fire."

He took a step closer, and the fire revealed his horrible appearance... His clothes were glued to his skin, and the congealed blood had started to stink!...

"Allah's mercy upon us, there's so much blood! Are you bleeding from an injury?"

"I don't know, I couldn't tell, it's totally soaked ..."

One by one, the mother removed her injured son's soiled clothes, searching for the wound, and found it on the left side of his chest... It had almost closed but could be seen as a diagonal line across his discolored skin... A few drops of blood had congealed and hardened below his chest and the edges of his wound looked black... The old woman stared long at that stab wound, and with her long years of experience, she knowingly shook her head...

"It's cold," broke the wounded son's voice and, as he put on a new shirt, he approached the fire...

Seated across the way, his mother watched him and kept still. The wrinkles on her mean old face furrowed even deeper, and her heart quaked with surprising anguish and rage...

Then, she got to her feet, stumbled over to the bandages hanging from the wall and unfolded them. She selected some herbs and prepared a tonic for her son, while she also smeared some balm on an old scrap of *yazma*.

"Ooooph...oooph," her son finally spoke, as these various cures began to revive him. "It was a long tough day... We fought until nightfall... That damned village put up a fight."

"Allah's mercy is great..."

"Anyway, all the villages have now been leveled to the ground, the people killed, and their homes reduced to ashes... Every time my blade cut through a *giaour*'s throat, the blood spouted like a fountain. We were fighting face to face, hand to hand, and I only ever used my gun on the ones that tried to get away..."

Their conversation continued this way for some time... The fire was going out. The old woman unrolled the kilims on the floor, and they lay down to sleep. She couldn't fall asleep as she lay there anxious about her son's rapid, noisy breathing.

Suddenly, a ragged voice sounded in the still of the night... And then some unclear, confused words. Her son was delirious, and, in his feverish sleep, he was reliving every grim moment he had experienced on that horrific day... In his nightmare, he took turns being the attacker one moment and the victim the next... Sometimes, he changed his voice, eerily mimicking his victims' screams.

The old woman heard it all and something like dread made its way into her knobby limbs. It was not only that she was worried about her son's condition, but also that terror was enclosing her soul. At that instant, the patient sat up and pleaded in his raspy voice, "*Anneh... Anneh*, I'm cold..."

Safiyeh had not heard that voice for some time… That was her son's childhood voice, and the voice of motherly care rang out, "*Oghloom… oghloom…* You're in so much pain… *oghloom…* May Allah have mercy on us…"

She had never felt such anguish in her life… It was as though the unshed tears for the deaths of her husband and father rushed to her eyes, suffocating her… She came to her son's side and could tell in the dark that his whole body was trembling… His teeth were chattering, and he could not speak. His wolflike eyes glowed in the dark. The old woman rushed to light some twigs dipped in resin. When she turned around, her son was sitting up on the kilim and, with one hand clasping his chest, he seemed to be choking as he vomited violently. Blood spurted from his mouth and nostrils, and, as though he was in the throes of death, his eyes began to glaze over. Safiyeh was quick and quiet as she attended to her son. Her limbs had regained the agility of her youth, but when he settled down, she could not bring herself to sleep and sat cross-legged by his side.

"*Anneh*, I'm much better, I would've choked if I hadn't vomited up the blood."

But his mother did not share his optimism, and the eyes in her wrinkled face blazed with renewed passion…

Until that point, she had avoided enquiring into the identity of her son's attacker, and the wounded victim had not mentioned it. But, at that moment, rage made her cry out, "Tell me, if the person who hurt you was a great hero, tell me, and I'll say, 'Good for him!' But if he was just a lowlife, tell me his name and I'll go find that son of a bitch and squash him under my own two feet. And if he's already dead and rotting, I'll dig up his grave with my nails and toss out his bones."

And that is when her son began to sing the praises of his enemy. And the more he extolled his courage, the greater grew his pride.

"I fought that *fedayi** all day, but my dagger was powerless against him, and my bullets kept missing … He was the one rousing the villagers against us, calling them to come and fight, and he never lost heart when they were defeated. He just sped ahead of us to another

---

*. Guerrilla fighter. (Tr.)

village... He was as tall as me, as burly too. He was so perfectly beautiful that all I wanted to do was watch him, and I couldn't bring myself to attack ... He was as brave as any Muslim I know. He walked through hails of bullets like a saint... One look at him made our men feel hopeless and weak, even though he refused to attack us. He tried to spare us, as though he was protecting his own life!... If there'd been just five other *fedayi* like him, they would've won."

He fell silent for a moment, coughed, and tasted once more the blood welling into his mouth.

"*Anneh*, I'm thirsty... My throat's dry, and it feels like horses are stampeding through my pounding ears."

Safiyeh took a clay jug, removed its lid of leaves, and offered it to her son. He drank it in one gulp, and then panting, almost breathless, he returned the jug, rested for a moment, and continued.

"All the houses had burned down, the *millet* destroyed... Nothing was left breathing where we'd been, but *he* wasn't killed. Heavy with loot and exhausted, the Muslims were returning to their villages, when I spotted him in the distance. He was riding over the hillsides, head held high and alone. If I'd shot at him, I might have missed, and he would've gotten away. So, I put my horse in a gallop and reached him ten minutes later. When he heard the approaching hooves, he turned around and waited for me. His eyes were calm and sad, and he was moving slowly.

'Hey, you son of a slave,' I shouted, 'come here and fight if you have a shred of courage!'

He was calm and as still as a statue. So, I jumped down from my horse, furious at the insult, and I charged at him. Our bodies locked together as we fought, his heart beating against my chest, mine against his... His arms were as hard as steel, but I managed to free my arm for a second, brought my dagger up and slashed his face at an angle. The blood blinded him, but he grabbed my arm as he fell and pulled me down with him. In a split second, his other hand stuck a small knife into my chest, and it went all the way in, up to the handle, as though I was just a mound of sand... My head began to spin, and I passed out. When I came to, we were lying in each other's arms, me and his corpse. I came to my knees and tried to wrench myself out of his grip. But it took a long time... That's what happened."

The darkness in the village grew thicker, and, weary from recounting these events, the wounded man slept a troubled sleep. The old woman remained by his side, sitting cross-legged and watching over him. And from time to time, when she felt her son's forehead, she found that either he was burning up or he was drenched in ice-cold sweat.

In his delirium, her son's lips began to quiver once more. But, this time, his voice sounded like another's and intoned with a tragically sweet cadence.

"He's my only child, don't kill him, please... You have the power, you and your sword, let him go... Have mercy like the Almighty and grant me my child's life... I'll be your slave, the dirt beneath your feet, but spare him, please..."

All at once, as though moved by something visceral rising from the pits of her soul, Safiyeh cried out, "*Oghloom*, you did spare him, didn't you? You did spare him!"

Her feverish son responded to his own mother just as he had responded to the Armenian mother.

"Life is wasted on you, you don't deserve this land and sky... Allah has decided your fate and He put this weapon in my hands."

Profound silence followed these words, and the Armenian mother's pleading voice could be heard once more on the wounded man's lips.

"Kill as many as you want, but kill me first so that I don't have to see him die... Don't crush a mother's heart. Have pity, let me die first... My body ached to give him life and trembled to see him grow, and now, every bit of me hurts when I watch his pain. Beware a mother's curse... Your time will come one day, and my son's corpse will snatch you by the ankles and drag you down with him into the grave... Spare him, please, he's only a child, he's innocent, just a little ray of light..."

"*Oghloom*, you did spare him, didn't you? You spared him!"

"It was even redder and even warmer than I thought when it spouted all over me, *anneh*, the blood of the Armenian child..."

At dawn, the whole village was anxious and met to deliberate. Even the most potent remedies proved to be ineffective, and Safiyeh's son was in the throes of death, unconscious and wheezing for three days. His ragged breathing made a din as loud as a drill digging for water. It could be heard from a distance. When his body began to lose heat, they wrapped the ailing man in layers of sheepskin, which were still warm from the animals that had been freshly slaughtered in vain. He seemed to be fighting for his life as his body writhed with horrible contortions. In his delirium, he no longer spoke, but the images of all his crimes seemed to move, in quick succession, across his glazed, terror-stricken eyes.

Safiyeh could not come to terms with his death, when it finally happened... Her wild, unfathomable maternal love compelled her to believe that she could labor anew to bring him back to life. And all through the night, as the villagers who had gathered in her hut fell asleep wherever they could lay their heads, she implored Allah stubbornly with her plaintive prayers, "Kill me first, so that I don't live to see him die... I'll be the dust on the ground... I'll be the lowliest of slaves, but spare my only child, please... My child's life is in your hands, won't you please grant me that? Have pity on his youth, let it shine like the sun, and turn your wrath upon me."

And Safiyeh failed to realize that her lips were repeating, almost word for word, the anguished pleas of an Armenian mother.

The New Bride

Peace was reinstated, and indignant hearts were regaining their former calm. The village had almost forgotten its many days of fury and murder and was gradually returning to normalcy.

Even those with imprisoned or exiled relations in distant dungeons or fortresses felt their worries subside. As had so many others, they too would doubtless eventually return and, before year's end, they would all entirely forget about that bloody nightmare.

If any unpunished criminals ever acknowledged their actions, everyone would react with shock and horror, compelled to believe that an evil demon had deafened and blinded them during those incidents. Because, before then, hadn't they all lived like brothers and sisters with their neighbors of a foreign race? Didn't they eat from the same bowl, drink from the same cup? And hadn't many of them broken bread together…?

But those moments of recognition were brief, and all their thoughts would instantly jumble into confusion. They had so fully appropriated the looted belongings that it no longer crossed their minds to distinguish between what was theirs and what had been attained through fire and blood. The women decorated themselves with the jewelry of murdered Armenian women, with bracelets wrenched from the arms of half-dead girls. Gold-chained necklaces adorned their arms and breasts, and one could even see, here and there, crimson drops of hyacinth and beautiful green flashes of emerald that had been stolen from the vessels of sacred sites.

They had also forgotten about the ruins, notwithstanding the vast field of ashes that grew like an incurable, embarrassing sore just next to the village. They had forgotten that there had been a time when their own hands had set fire to those fields, to those peaceful habitats and that in their frenzy, they had fallen upon the neighboring *millet* like a horde of demons. They had incited each other, excelled each other in their violence and zeal. And, once drunk on the spilled blood and dazzled by all the loot, their hearts had run dry of human feelings.

But now, people refuted and denied the destruction committed at their own hands. Peace had been reinstated and the *zooloom* was receding into the past, fading into the fog of oblivion. The village, which was flush with loot, was starting to worry about what tomorrow would bring, and that is why murderous hands were already reaching for their hoes and spades.

***

That morning, Selimeh woke up with contractions. Her husband and mother-in-law had already left at dawn to work in the fields. She was alone and an irrepressible sadness cast a shadow over her hopes of imminent motherhood. She got up and looked around across the rooftop. With the cotton harvest ready to be picked, all the village girls and women were away working in the nearby fields. A still silence reigned all around. The sun was rising into the dome of heaven, flooding the world with its rays. It blinded Selimeh, and she closed her eyes. Her knees were buckling, and unfathomable fatigue drained all her strength. She assessed her situation with the typical pique of someone in her state. She was beset by ill fortune. She looked ugly and skinny. Her normally thick head of hennaed hair, with locks cascading down her back, had almost entirely fallen out. Her face once glowed with rosy cheeks... Where were they now...? Where had they vanished to, the spark in her eyes, the liveliness of that plump peasant woman with some meat on her bones? Her arms weak, her legs wobbly, all that was left of her was a shadow of her previous self...! Had someone cast a curse upon her...? The contractions overwhelmed her momentarily... She wanted to scream, but the pervading silence prevented her. She waited for the pain to pass, and holding on to the rickety railing, she struggled to make her way down from the roof.

Selimeh was a new bride. Shortly before the events, she had married the bravest, most fearless young man of the village. He had fought like a tiger during the incidents. His renowned courage had exhilarated her terribly, and she had eagerly awaited his return.

Like so many others, her husband had also returned with a heavy load of loot. They had it made now, they were rich. Their pathetic little cottage was full of beautiful things befitting of a Muslim. Their feet could not touch the ground because their dirt floor was covered with colorful carpets. And Selimeh had also felt that, when he returned from the fighting, her husband's love was raging like a blaze. Breathless impatience and feverish excitement had agitated her, like a fire stoked by the wind, as though death had arrived upon their threshold...

At first, Selimeh's husband had aroused her pride, but then, he began to terrify her. Day by day, her heart grew more estranged. At night, she watched him sleep. And as his horrible nightmares made him gasp, toss, and turn, a vague and violent compulsion stirred within her. She felt an urge to inflict harm. As he conquered her with his caresses, her body would nonetheless resist, and her repulsion would drive her mad. She felt that there was something pernicious in his passion. She could sometimes hear cries of abuse and affrontery reach her through her husband's prickly kisses. And the pupils of his staring eyes, the riveted pupils of a predator would train on her, just as they had surely trained on the bleeding victims of those terrible events.

A cold sweat drenched Selimeh's body, and she sought to dispel these alien sentiments from her mind. Her pregnancy had been difficult and painful. She had been carrying a curse, not a baby in her womb...! It felt like countless bloodthirsty fangs were shredding her insides. Each contraction made her want to run away, and, as though she was caught in a nightmare, she paced around the confining cottage until she collapsed from exhaustion... She would sometimes stand on their threshold and gaze upon the village bathed in sunlight. The day was so very long...! They would not return from the fields until much later. It felt as though heaven and earth had come to a standstill in the scorching heat. It was difficult to breathe. Her eyes blurred, and a peculiar drowsiness veiled reality, pulling it away from the young woman's consciousness.

A confusion of fragmentary memories returned to her tormented mind. She could see her husband in drunken nights of passion as he compelled her to wear all that cursed jewelry. Pale as a corpse, she indulged his whims. But she always adamantly refused to wear the diadem that had belonged to a new bride... Among all the thousands who had shed their blood, the blood of that one adolescent bride had tormented her like the fires of hell...

"Allah as my witness," her husband used to shout, "she was as beautiful as the light... And I killed her for you because I wanted you to have all this gold..."

At first, she had felt a heavy, oppressive sadness upon seeing those ornaments. It was as though the new bride's spirit had come and stood in the path her life would take. She could sometimes see her as she must have appeared during festivities, her bashful brow veiled beneath the shadow cast by her kerchief, her large eyes cheerful with childlike joy, the light playing with the smile on her lips... But, at other times, she would assume an entirely different appearance, as though she was overcome with terror. A brutish murderous hand would be snatching the bridal ornament from her cadaverous forehead. And there would be a conflagration dancing on the horizon, while men raging with irreconcilable hatred and howling like beasts annihilated one another...

***

Selimeh wanted to forget all that and to turn her attention to her hopes of motherhood... In just a few hours, she would hear her baby's cry. She felt a violent surge of tenderness in her heart and the contractions became more bearable. Like a lioness, she would defend its life against all sorts of trials and tribulations. She defied the curses heaped upon them but was terrified at the thought that the diadem might bring her infant bad luck... And she resolved to crush it beneath her feet, to grind it into ashes and dust...

When she attempted to stand up, a gentle touch on her shoulder seemed to tug at her. Selimeh found herself face to face with the spirit of the murdered new bride... For several long and agonizing minutes, she fought against its ethereal, menacing strength... Her limbs cramped as she did her utmost to resist. Her screams caught in her throat, the tongue between her clenching teeth turned black and petrified, and a foamy drool ran down her chest. Fits of pain knocked her down, until, defeated and faint, she collapsed onto the carpet...

When she came to, she was weak and infirm. Crawling along the floor for fear of waking the spiteful ghost, she approached a drawer, and opened it. She removed the diadem wrapped in a *yazma* and managed to reach their threshold. The fresh air and light revived her. Her contractions had abated appreciably, and the evening breeze cooled the sweat on her temples. At last, she unwrapped the *yazma* and looked long and hard at the golden diadem. As her gaze lingered, she felt a growing upsurge of emotions. She had been very wealthy and beautiful, and of course, it was her fiancé who had bestowed his betrothed with that gift. Selimeh held it in her fingers and raised it to her eyes. Suddenly, she felt shivers down her spine. A few strands of hair still adhered to the ornament. They were long, as fine as silk and shone like gold in the sunlight... Before she knew it, Selimeh's lips were muttering the words, "My sister, my sister..."

Which beautiful head had that diadem adorned? What happy occasion had prompted that gift? How had that head full of hopes and dreams been so guilty as to provoke the heavy blows of a murderous hand? Had her adolescent body burned in the flames, or had it been stabbed and mutilated, left to rot in the sun on a deserted road?

"My sister... my sister..."

And with her head leaning to one side, Selimeh wept for some time.

***

When the villagers returned much later from the cotton fields, they found Selimeh. Her skin had turned black, and it seemed that she had been strangled. Her limbs were stiff with a stony chill. The open drawer and scattered jewelry provoked all kinds of speculation, but the true nature of Selimeh's pain did not cross anyone's mind. And no one gave a thought to her desperate struggles or to her terror as she lay dying. Only when her grieving husband approached to bid his bride farewell and lifted her shroud to see her deathly face did he think of the new bride murdered at his hand and mumbled, "Allah as my witness, she was as beautiful as the light, so dazzling that I had to kill her. But, in the shadow of death, you can hardly tell them apart..."

All at once, he felt the lingering pain of prickles creeping up his spine. Unable to resist their overwhelming strength, his lean scrawny body began to writhe like a snake.

The Glory

The autumn dusk faded swiftly over the vast plains. Great shadows emerged from bare expanses of harvested fields, soaring overhead like mythical winged creatures, while coppery rays of light that had burst across the sky slowly began to dim. The leafless silhouettes of distant trees were barely visible in the thickening darkness, and tight clumps of dense thickets seemed poised for the impending arrival of a mysterious night.

One could still hear a few cowherds dawdling in the local pastures as they sounded their sad lingering lows. A cart creaked by. And, while shepherds ensconced securely amid their bleating flocks replied with their own soft bleats, the villagers rushed to conclude their day's work, because, in not too long, the muezzin's voice would resound from the top of the village's wooden minaret.

A group of veiled adolescent girls were returning from the stream bearing brimming jugs of water on their shoulders. Crickets were chirping and, just as weary ploughmen were slowing their pace to exchange a few words on their way home, they were interrupted by the sweet, drawn-out song of the melancholy evening call to prayer.

After performing the *namaz*,[*] Mustafa *dayi*[†] and his wife had their dinner sitting cross-legged on the rolled-out floor mats of their little mud house. Despite their advanced age, they both still seemed strong and lively. Their eldest, Suleyman, had left years ago to serve in the military, and their younger sons earned their wages by working for nearby farms. The couple's combined efforts sufficed to cultivate their lands... Praise Allah, their crops were always bountiful, their land produced a thousand times more than they ever hoped, their livestock were healthy, fat, and sturdy and a velvety green coated their pastures... The elderly couple ate quietly, but they contemplated at length about all this and, they were so sure of their identical sentiments that they conveyed their replies with the simple exchange of a knowing glance. Occasionally, a muffled lowing from the adjacent barn would accompany their thoughts. And,

---

*. Prayer. (Tr.)
†. Uncle. (Tr.)

sometimes, their thoughts would fall quiet. A sense of indescribable contentment would come over them, not unlike the sickly torpor exuded in the heavy, musky breaths of domesticated animals.

They had been born, bred, and brought up in that village, and they knew no other horizon but its vast plains. Once a year, the husband would head out to the sparse bushy woodlands nearby and come back with a year's worth of wood piled onto his cart. As the only noteworthy incident in their lives, they recalled the death of the "fair little one," which had suddenly dropped dead as though it had been felled by an axe. The poor ox had been a victim of the evil eye. So, with much faith and fervor, they had doubled and tripled the number of protective charms and blue beads that they normally fastened to their livestock's necks and heads. They looked festive when they went off to graze and their tiny trinkets always tinkled merrily.

They were their pride and joy, their burden and their darlings. They had received more care perhaps than their four sons, who were left to their own devices like a litter of pups, but who had grown up tall and healthy... Did anyone dare imply that Mustafa *dayi* did not relish hearing others praise his eldest? He was the picture of his own youth, and there was no other like him in the whole village. He was brave and handsome. Who had ever seen the likes of him? As tall as a poplar tree with an unbreakable back, arms of steel, eagle eyes and a clear complexion? When he would throw his rifle over his shoulder and mount his horse to go hunting in the woods, you could not tell him apart from a legendary hero or a spirit headed for conquest. Birds in flight or rabbits on the run could not escape his aim, and his gun had never missed. When he was finally old enough for military service, his parents suggested that they pay the *bedel*[*] so that he could stay home. But Suleyman dismissed the idea with contempt. Was he a new bride that he should stay at home? Was he expected to wash his mother's veils instead of going off and becoming a man? His hands and feet could grip as firmly as ever, his eyes were sharp, and his heart was stout. And so, one morning, man and wife went to the edge of their village to see off the new recruits. They all displayed courage, and the village had no

---

[*]. A sum paid for exemption from military service. (Tr.)

shortage of brave men. But who could deny that Suleyman was exceptional? Everyone seemed to have forgotten their own sons and derived all their pride and solace from him. And as the caravan of new recruits advanced along the long winding roads in the distance, they could still see the red *yazma* tied to his fez as its fluttering tips seemed to wave farewell.

"Glory to Allah, glory to you," and his mother's eyes would dampen with tears of joy… "You are leaving in glory; may you return in glory. May your arms never know defeat."

***

Mustafa *dayi* was sitting outside their cottage door smoking his *choobook** and thinking of his faraway son, when across the way in the dappled shade, he saw the brows of a pair of white oxen advancing toward him, slowly pulling a cart laden with wood. It belonged to Haydar *agha*,† who had left for the nearby town the previous day.

"*Merhaba*…!"‡

With his hand on his chest, Mustafa *dayi* received the greeting and asked straightaway with some surprise, "Didn't you sell any of your wood?"

Exhausted, Haydar *agha* sat on the ground. Despite the cool weather, his sweaty face looked somewhat distressed. His eyes wandered and he hesitated to speak. Suddenly a deep and long-suppressed sigh rose from his breast.

"Oooph… oooph…*dayi*, such awful times, such black days."

"God help us, *oghool*** …," trembling himself. The *choobook* had fallen from his limp hand onto his lap, and he could feel his wife's labored breathing behind him.

Haydar came to his knees, leaned his head toward them and, showing the dim distant horizon with his hand, he muttered through his teeth, "*Harb*,†† there's a war…"

---

*. Tobacco pipe. (Tr.)
†. A term of address. (Tr.)
‡. Hello. (Tr.)
**. Son. (Tr.)
††. War. (Tr.)

They were quiet for a moment and the good-natured, naïve expressions of their creaturely eyes strayed in the dark of night.

All through the night, man and wife were unable to sleep, and at the first light of dawn, they went straight to the imam to learn more about the events. The old woman struggled to walk and wept.

"*Oghloom*, where are you at this moment, in which of our hills and dales…? Will I ever see you again, standing as tall as a poplar tree…?"

Mustafa *dayi* maintained his composure and laughed through his whiskers.

"Why are you fretting, woman? What're you afraid of? Suleyman is strong and brave. We had our turn at it, in our time. It's not as though everyone who goes to war ends up dead…!"

After days and weeks of peace and quiet, the village was now deeply unsettled, like a lake swept by evil winds. *Harb…!* The reserves are called in, villagers are on the run, many withdraw into the mountains, taking their animals with them… The tearful eyes of mothers and orphans, faces struck with confusion and madness.

Accompanied by other elderly villagers, Mustafa *dayi* went to the nearby town several times awaiting news as he huddled in a corner of the train station. They lived like blind men fumbling through darkness and uncertainty. People arriving from the capital could have brought them some news, but their eyes watched as the only trains that came down from the villages were those filled with reserves and new recruits. And they passed through without making a stop at the station…

"There's a war, *harb*, and the spilled blood is flooding our lands…!"

What can one tell the women asking after their beloveds and children? Lips have gone mute, no one will utter a word. The villagers could not suppress the great resentments awakening within them as an endless succession of trains coming down from the villages distressed them with their thundering approach, their hissing steam engines, their red lights blazing at dusk, their sharp piercing whistles. They were wracked with anxiety.

But it was just as difficult to remain in the village. Wringing their hands, their eyes glued to the road, they would wait. The rains had come, and the soil was pliant, but no one had any mind to plough and seed… How many mouths would they have left to feed? Let us see if they would have any luck from the next harvest. Ploughmen would neglect their work and gather in coffeehouses to distract themselves from their anxious wait. They would discuss previous wars, in which some of them had also fought. And they would invoke the heroic historic names of their glorious military conquests. But the women remained impassive to that self-indulgence. Sitting cross-legged, they beat their knees with their hands and thought of their brave men, whose veins were being sliced open perhaps at that very instant.

***

One early morning, they noticed the first caravan of refugees. Long lines of carriages covered with straw mats advanced slowly along the entire length of the road and brought with them the first inklings of unfortunate news. Gloomy, hopeless sorrow eclipsed their hearts when suddenly there was a flash of joy. The village men had fought like lions. Their outstanding courage and daring were on everyone's lips. Some had been martyred, but many had been injured and escaped, awaiting their turn to return to their native lands. The village imam heartened and encouraged them. He had heard it all from a credible source, and there was no reason to doubt him. As for Suleyman…! Ooph… ooph… Glory to his parents and to his fatherland.

Leaning on an elm tree, Mustafa *dayi* and his wife were giddy with joy. They felt as though they were dreaming, and, in their excitement, they started planning, right then and there, a welcome reception for Suleyman. They knew that he had been hurt, that it was critical, but that he would recover. If God had saved him from enemy attack, why wouldn't he protect him now…? And they assumed that on the day of his return, all the nearby farms and all the villagers would rejoice. Mustafa *dayi* knew just what to do. The hunting rifles hanging on their walls could not be left idle on that day. Bullets would thunder not in ones and twos, but in the hundreds.

"*Aman, oghloom,*" his mother would say, her chest puffed with pride, "our darkest days are bright again, may the whole world be your just reward."

Comforted somewhat now in their state of misery, the villagers waited patiently. From morning until night, endless caravans of refugees passed along the main road. Sometimes, when the autumn skies brightened, they would stop, light a fire, and spend the night in the woods. Fair-haired, bright-eyed Rumelian children would walk all the way to the village, asking for work of any kind. That is when the locals would learn all the horrible details which sent long shivers up their spines and inflamed their enduring sorrows, their deep-seated resentments.

One gray, rainy evening, they noticed some battered, ramshackle carts trailing behind refugees rushing towards them. The women approached them and waited with a vague sense of dread constricting their hearts. The carts turned off the road, entered the grassy field and stopped. A series of rainstorms had made the roads impassable. Groups of people dismounted. Were they bringing *moohajeers** to the village? But, no, they looked more like phantoms, bent low, emaciated, walking aimlessly. As though they were drunk or on the verge of death. The closer they came, the more shocking they looked. Their movements seemed unwilled, and they wandered around as though they were blind. They had the terrified appearance of fever-stricken men pursued by a perpetual nightmare. Still and staring, the old women observed them, while the younger ones succumbed to feelings of contempt and revulsion. Suddenly, one of them left the group and rushed ahead. Dressed in rags, he straightened his back and walked on trembling legs with a threatening, sinister air… Allah…! The terrified women wanted to flee when a voice, fierce and defiant, rose suddenly from their midst, "Suleyman, *oghloom*…!"

They had been deserted and left to starve for days. Nothing, not even a rock, could have survived that fate. When they managed to speak, they had so much to tell. They had turned on each other, torn at each other to quench the hellish thirst burning their feverish lips with a drop of blood… And they were no longer men reuniting with their parents, but rather ghosts that had escaped from their graves. Luckiest were those whose jaundiced, cadaverous lips drooped and drooled, incapable of

---

*. Refugees. (Tr.)

expressing the words to recount the details of the inferno that had consumed them.

Although the villagers who gathered in coffeehouses gloated less ardently than before about their great fighters, they continued to extol them, inevitably relaying their heroic exploits to succeeding generations. They eventually overcame the horror induced by the returning men, and the intoxication of glory made them forget the truth. Only the women, and the mothers especially, were unable to grasp why and how the men could continue to boast. And, as they fixed their eyes on the specters of their loved ones, they wondered whether all that talk about glory wasn't just a terrible joke. That was how they tried to console themselves as mothers whose broken hearts had suffered the cruelest torments.

—1914—

ԱԶԱՏԱՄԱՐՏ

AZATAMARD

ՕՐԱԹԵՐԹ

ԹՈՒՐՔ ԿՆՈՋ ԱԶԱՏԱԳՐՈՒԹԵԱՆ ՀԱՐՑԸ

ՄԻՈՒԹԵԱՆ ԿՈՂ ԱՆԳԼԻԱԿԱՆ Բ

On the Question of Turkish Women's Emancipation

One of the most important and pressing questions in Turkey today concerns the emancipation of Turkish women.

We cannot fail to address it in our judgments about the state of humanity, no matter how specific or generalized they may be. Because if the pioneering status of the country's Christian women is to exert its inevitable influence – and has indeed already done so among the customs of Muslim women –, then, by the same token, it is impossible to even imagine that any changes among the great totality of Turkish women will be without consequence for us.

Before delving into the main topic, it might not be unwarranted to mention that opponents of such an obviously just and plain cause often assert the impracticability of those ambiguous, unclear, extremist demands that are so incompatible with the physiological condition of women, and which bear the general title of *'feminism.'* At the moment, that poor word has become so laughable and is labeled with so many contradictory, meaningless, debatable, and, importantly, crude declarations and demands, that it is imperative to clarify just what we mean when we speak of women's emancipation.

In its simplest and most illuminating form, it is, above all else, the cause in defense of humanity's inalienable rights. Woman, being a person, has rights and responsibilities. Her individuality and all the possible variations of its expression must reach their apex. Any external obstacles or pressures against their unimpeded evolution cannot be tolerated. And already in civilized countries, the question of women's emancipation has gradually ceased to be the collective demands of one of the sexes and has become yet another feature of a broader social struggle. If in some countries, legal obstacles exist that bar women from entering specific professions, they constitute obstacles that are so devoid of significance, both in a general and a specific sense, that they are not worth sighing about or engaging in debates.

All branches of the arts and the great work of education are now open as professions for all the women of this world and, for the moment, that can already be deemed enough. We can definitively assert that a set of major, fundamental obstacles that once used to violate the social rights of women, hindering their free and full development have now been overcome. Every woman can reach the pinnacle of her capabilities. Obstacles are not inconquerable, and they can only conquer those who remain mediocre. Besides, mediocrities among both sexes and in all classes have nothing valuable to offer anyway.[*]

But Turkey occupies a unique place with its obstructionist laws targeting Muslim women specifically. If, in other countries, family and social customs and prejudices continue to restrict women's actions, impeding their freedom and relegating them to a perpetual state of inferiority, we can perceive nonetheless that there are no serious and fundamentally obstructionist obstacles. If a woman can disregard those prejudices and customs; if a woman possesses the requisite strength and has an awareness of her intrinsic power; and if she can liberate herself from those countless trivial obstacles, which hem her in like a web, she can become absolutely free. Only Turkish women find themselves in a position where they must struggle against not only stagnant, centuries-old customs, but also against the country's laws. That is why, whereas in other countries, women's emancipation is one facet of broader social struggles, in Turkey, it is a question of governance. If in other countries, women striving for emancipation must confront the resistance of their parents, husbands, and relatives, Turkish women also have, in addition to all these, the police as well.

As a result, half the Turkish race exists in a state of paralysis. Turkish women are reduced to being an incompetent, immature, and confined constituent, unable to perform any active role in the many tasks that are crucial for their fatherland. By contrast, they pose an obstacle in times of serious and fundamental reforms: rather than being a source of support, they constitute a heavy yoke that prevents all progress in the steps being taken toward civilization.

---

[*]. It is almost degrading for genuinely strong women working in technology or other sectors to be valued on the basis of their sex. That amounts to an appreciation merely of one's relative worth. (Au.)

Turkish women's rudimentary efforts and initiatives,* which are extremely praiseworthy attempts and deserving of all encouragement, are also, however, inadequate for casting off such a heavy yoke. There is a real need for serious, fundamental, unflagging, and organized action, especially in the education sector, towards the attainment of victory through an ultimate awakening. I do not wish here to name names, but I do know of many estimable, educated, and passionate Muslim women, who can assume the leadership of such a national movement. The absence of sociality is the reason that those valuable forces remain dispersed and siloed. But the day that they finally risk every sacrifice (and I mean, *every* sacrifice) to create a solid nucleus of resistance, they will have all women at their side, and the movement will become invincible. The drive to be free from one's bonds must be as powerful as those bonds. And, in their struggle, Turkish women can draw on the aid of something endowed by the tyrants themselves: namely, the absolutely insufferable yoke that is foisted upon them.

Indeed, the realities of Turkish women perceived by our habituated eyes are galling and horrifying. The whole of Muslim womanhood is bearing the weight of the heaviest restrictions. Turkish women have been subjected to men's sovereignty by being deprived not only of their innermost psychological and intellectual rights, but also even in the realm of their most mundane daily activities. They are the perpetually veiled. Their dress – which should, in principle, only have to obey aesthetic norms and their own preferences – is subjected to the strictest police scrutiny. They cannot reveal their faces whenever or however they want. They cannot, without eliciting outrage and provoking government involvement, make any alterations to the mandated dress code. The Sheikh-ul-Islam makes frequent pronouncements on that topic: "Muslim women are forbidden from wearing *ferajeh*s in this or that style; we command that all who remain intransigent must receive the severest punishment." And there have even been occasions when venerable officers serving on military tribunals rendered verdicts against

---

*. Periodicals aimed exclusively at women, women's groups, etc. (Au.)

such intransigent Muslim women over some detail or other regarding their dress.[*]

Although all these restrictions do not fundamentally prevent the natural course of things, and young Muslim women often succeed, without transgressing the imposed mandates, in satisfying their appetites for all the newest fashion and accessories, the reality does not cease to be galling and categorically insulting to the most human sentiments of Turkish women, who receive a European upbringing on the one hand, while, on the other, they must veil themselves.

The insult often assumes a cruel and violent form when the issue concerns other restrictions. Muslim women are forbidden from associating with men in public, from riding in the same car, etc., if that man does not belong to the circle of permissible relations dictated by law (father, brother, husband). But how can one establish the permissibility of a stranger's status at just one glance? As a result, any careless police officer has the right to subject law-abiding citizens to the most offensive interrogation. Each and every Muslim woman, regardless of whether she is the mother of multiple children, a faithful spouse, or a pure, adolescent girl, can come under suspicion. The law and the government deny her the complete trust, which is indispensable to the conduct of entirely good and refined mores.

Turkish women's domestic life no longer holds any secrets. A great deal has been written about it and we know – leaving aside its discussion in literary serials and novels – that in reality, it represents the gloomiest, dreariest, and most menacing environment on earth, replete with the most profound and hidden miseries. We do not have the space here for a detailed discussion, but suffice it to recall that behind those solitary, silent, and dark cages live groups of thinking, feeling, and wretched creatures who are enduring intolerable tyrannies; and, suffice it to momentarily turn our thoughts to those profound feelings of hatred, to those blandishments, artifices, treacheries, and, especially, to all the

---

[*]. Some Cabinets consisting of various political parties gave the highest priority to immediately making declarations regarding the specifications of Turkish women's dress code. And it was the liberal side that showed the greatest zeal. This awful show of fervor is a telling fact. (Au.)

suffering and pain, that make us shudder with the realization that the question of Turkish women's emancipation is now a matter of urgency.

When tyranny is so unjust and so absolute that the oppressed are compelled to feel justified when they indiscriminately exploit the very first available opportunity to help themselves, then all moral foundations can be deemed compromised; and so, even if not everything may be forgiven, everything nevertheless becomes possible.

Orientalists and foreigners in distant lands who do not share the cruel fate of Turkish women often perceive a certain beauty in their lot. A veiled woman is always alluring; the harem attracts discriminating tastes in search of something different. But can a garment be thought beautiful when it represents the stamp of servitude? Can a dwelling be deemed captivating when it bears such a strong likeness to a prison?

Before closing, I want to offer a reminder that the emancipation of Turkish women is not fundamentally contradictory to the religion of Islam;* and that a deviation from its original motives has led to the institution of those arbitrary, torturous, and distrustful living conditions in which the natural development of an entire race's female population is sinking. They represent one of the most beautiful, capable, admirable, and sensitive examples of womanhood in this world, and they are, moreover, uniquely gifted. Yet, they suffer under a yoke the likes of which exist nowhere else on earth and in our times.

---

*. A series of sharia laws that are currently in effect demonstrate the high status that Islam grants to women. The laws endowing them with proprietary, marriage, custodial, and inheritance rights all underwrite the freedom of women. One could devote a separate article to discussing those topics. (Au.)

The *Namehram*: Life as a Turkish Woman

The famous feminist and renowned writer, Mrs. Maria Szeliga,[*] once asked a Turkish notable – at the time, an exile, but today a high-ranking imperial functionary – what it is that renders the condition of Turkish women so exceptional and their emancipation almost impossible.

"The *namehram*…," he replied. "If we approach the issue head on and remain unperturbed by the ensuing controversy, the question of Turkish women's emancipation can begin taking its normal course in our society only when the *namehram* is lifted."

And, just what is that oppressive custom that plays such a wretched role in the lives of millions of human beings, by impeding their emotional and intellectual evolution, by posing an obstacle to every single aspiration and ascent, by obstructing all available opportunities and ultimately, like a chain tied around one's ankles, by weighing down every single movement by Turkish women toward emancipation?

Is it a fixed religious commandment? Or the antiquated fragment of traditional mores that had existed within the race? What basis does it have and how did it originate?

Opinions about the *namehram* are infinitely varied. And, if we take into account all the different statements that have been made about that issue, we will finally arrive at this conclusion: that the *nahemram* as it is implemented today is the result of unilaterally interpreted religious precepts which were compatible with practices that had already existed within the race; and although they were implemented more loosely or strictly at various times, their institutionalization over the years has transformed them into such a foundational and unshakable structure

*. Also known in France and the USA as Maria Chéliga or Chéliga Loevy (1854 – 1927). She was a Polish novelist, poet, and social publicist, as well as a socialist and pioneer of the international Polish women's movement. See *Biographical Dictionary of Women's Movements and Feminisms in Central, Eastern, and South Eastern Europe: 19th and 20th Centuries*, Eds. Francisa de Haan, Krasimira Daskalova, and Anna Toufi (Budapest: Central European University Press, 2006): 562 – 566. (Tr.)

that one cannot possibly overturn them without provoking fanaticism and inciting great agitation.

And yet, we know that in many areas – such as the villages, where the populace is much more devout and where Islam is preserved in all its simplicity and purity –, the *namehram* practically does not exist. Muslim peasant women work in the fields with their heads barely covered by a simple kerchief. They eat in the company of their relatives or neighbors. They accompany them, be it on horseback or on foot. They buy and sell, and, ultimately, their lifestyle does not differ definitively from the customs of Christian peasant women, contrary to the entrenched differences among urban-dwelling women of different religions. Similarly, in various other countries, such as Egypt, such as the Caucasus, Muslim women are not confined by the same restrictions and torturous laws, which seem to be unique to our capital city.

On the other hand, while abroad, I once had the opportunity to meet a Turkish philosopher, who insisted that the *namehram* was primarily a Byzantine custom; that it was carried over from Genesis into Islam – also resulting in the monstrous creation of the eunuch class; and, that the religious precepts relating to the isolation of women, to veiling, to curtailing men's temptations to go astray, do not differ much from similar precepts found in other religions. And if one takes a charitable, open-minded approach toward their justifications, they appear to be on a par with similar categories of religious precepts in Judaism and Christianity. Indeed, hadn't veiling, dressing plainly to show modesty also been the concerns of Christian women? But time and morality, as well as ideas about personal dignity could not become firm, solid laws; and besides, have the laws restricting Muslim women been absolutely effective? Is it possible to say that there is no great difference between the domestic, moral, public, etc. customs of Turkish women a hundred years ago and the ideas and practices of women today?

It seems to me that the important thing is to provide Turkish women with an explanation formulating the true worth of that primary, systematic, and fundamental restriction that is weighing them down. One must research its foundations, its history, and its transformations over time. Today, in its guise as a mysterious and inviolable law arising from religious origins, it has become a huge invincible barrier. One must approach it, examine its different points and peculiarities, acquaint oneself with its principles and aims, and perhaps then, it might become possible to accept that it, the *namehram*, is not so impregnable after all. And the onus to undertake that great task rests on the shoulders of Turkish women, of course.

Overall, foreign sociologists, women intellectuals, and philosophers had placed great hopes on that courageous and inclusive initiative, which the Young Turks – who were taking refuge in the great cities of Europe during the autocratic system – promised to enact. The latter never ceased to profess that the captive status of Turkish women was one aspect of the many evils perpetrated by the autocracy, and that once the bonds had been unchained, once the constitutional regime was established, the very first implemented reform would honor the civil rights of Turkish women.

But I will never forget Mrs. Szeliga's shock as she relayed to me the rage felt by some of her estimable Turkish acquaintances in response to the liberal conduct of Turkish women during the first days of euphoria.

"You had to see it to believe it, how they'd changed! And their outrage was so immense that they couldn't find the words to describe the conduct of those heretics. You must tell them, either in person or in a public statement, that they must give that spontaneous joy and excitement its due, given how long the majority of Turkish women have borne the yoke of so much suffering. The euphoria of these days will pass, and they'll regain their natural equilibrium. They should never resort to repressive measures. The objection that Muslim women are not deserving of or mature enough for liberation is wrong, merely the typical kind of rationalization employed by tyrants…"

To this day, however, the whole group of leading authorities – who, as individuals, claim to support women's emancipation, of course, and whose open-mindedness seems to be unencumbered by the bonds of prejudice – not only refuse to act in accordance with their personal convictions, but they also appear to be committed to achieving the contrary. Can one imagine, even for an instant, that the governing circles – who are always in contact with the great civilizations of Europe, were nourished on them and matured through them; who accept the importance of applying Western methods in all spheres of operation; who see that the West has penetrated into the deepest corners of the country with its manners, its customs, and every other element of its civilization – believed that women could remain exempt from that process of evolution by being confined within the fortifications of strict archaic codes? Can they deny that every one of those practices, which preclude the collaboration of men and women in the social sphere or in the educational, technological, or other sectors of employment, are immensely detrimental to the country's general progress? These conditions harm not only women, but also men. The captors and captives are pitched against each other like enemies. Families are formed in that kind of confrontational environment. When men are forced to live apart from women at a young age, they become coarse, uncouth. And they tend to regard women as decorative objects of pleasure – and nothing more. Even with respect to the nation's morale, it is imperative to maintain intimacy and collaboration between the sexes. Even children often lack the natural filial respect and reverence for their mothers that are characteristic of children in the West. When a Turkish boy employs a derisory, insulting attitude toward his mother, you can be sure that he is echoing his father's tone. The great influence of mothers, sisters, and close female relatives enables the race to mold its young into magnanimous, noble, and valiant men. It is not a demonstration of strength to trample upon all that is sacred; such a misconception is unique to tyrants.

Time is already playing its part in today's world. Efforts to preserve the outer shell can only provoke a single outcome: namely, rendering the conditions of Turkish women's lives even harsher and more intolerable. Modern ideas and sentiments have found their way into harems thanks to literature and art, and even more so due to the education of men and the ensuing changes in their models and ideals. Is it possible to conceive of a woman who would not aspire to those ideals of womanhood that are harbored by every young Europeanized Turkish man? The rise in marriages with foreign women demonstrates the prevailing inclinations within the race. Everyone, male and female, longs for light and freedom. We must fling open the doors and windows to let the sunlight flood those caged rooms and dispel the remaining shadows and darkness and damp.

There are thousands of beings whose hearts, feelings, and intelligence are now weary of fading and wasting away behind shadows and veils. They feel deserving of the best possible circumstances. They suffer as women and as mothers, and they consider their current status to be offensive. They want to demonstrate their capabilities, to develop them freely, and to contribute them to the affairs of public life. They want to live a free and valued existence; to be modest without coercion; to arouse respect without police intervention. They want to play their part for their race and for humanity, a role that is sure to be unique and beautiful. They want to express all of their accumulated energy and intellectual power, which have remained unemployed and gone to waste; often, in fact, undermining them by consuming and extinguishing their refined, sensitive souls like a candle.

I have sadly witnessed all too often the moment that a fair, thoughtful brow appears for an instant, only to be concealed beneath the black veil shrouding its face like everlasting mourning. I have perceived all too often the presence of a great, irrevocable sorrow and the regret of a wasted life in tearful, passionate eyes and on withered lips.

But we must turn our attention most of all to the misery endured by those, who have ceased to be objects of pleasure. They may have once been the crowning jewel of a harem, or perhaps of several harems, but they are approaching old age. They have been dismissed and forgotten. Their children are left to their own devices, scattered, unloved, and alone.[*] Ultimately, with reference to both rights and to humanity, the issue of Turkish women's emancipation represents a matter of urgency. Perhaps it is not too late for the day when everyone will agree to lift that black curtain, which has suppressed so many withering generations and deprived the Turkish race of their flowers and fruits.

---

[*] One cannot point to the stipends that must be paid by husbands who release their wives or by children to their elderly mothers. There are emotional and psychological factors that exceed financial needs. And besides, one cannot resolve the issue of released wives and mothers deprived of their children by treating them the same way as retired employees who are entitled to a pension. (Au.)

The Wait

'The three greatest torments in life are lack of sleep, unquenched thirst, and waiting.'

- An oriental proverb

Darkness looms over the city as autumn squalls drive gloomy plumes of heavy clouds across the pale moonlit sky. Doors are shut and shutters are drawn, and, in that hushed, desolate atmosphere, the neighborhoods seem to be uninhabited. As soon as the specter of a shadowy human figure appears behind a set of locked window bars, it disappears almost instantly back into the wan light glimmering from the deepest corners of cloistered rooms. No matter how much joy and misery reside within them, these homes are as silent as tombs and as unknowable as lifeless hearts.

A house that sits at the very edge of a distant neighborhood and faces a vast expanse of fresh colorful fields appears to be even bleaker, even quieter, even more neglected and desolate. But from the bars in its window, a light begins to flicker and seems to wait. That light glows every night and waits in vain.

The dark of night deepens, and silence lords over the vast fields. In the light behind those bars, a heart awaits with steadfast hope. Even its fantasies cannot disrupt the long hours of anxious anticipation in the absolute quiet of the still, solemn air.

***

Khalideh Hanum is now withered away. Her heavy make-up scarcely adheres to her pale, emaciated flesh. The long lines of her pencil-drawn eyes and smudged eyebrows create a pitiful expression as her face tenses with the anguish of her wait. Her warm, inviting room remains the same as ever, made cozy with rugs and the aroma of halva. But gone now are love and beauty. Where is her beloved, and why has he not returned? Year after year, every morning, hope springs anew in her gloomy heart and every day, she waits once more.

She is one of many women who have been released by their husbands. But she refuses to reconcile herself to that fact. Of course, her beloved will return just as he had left, his spurs urging his horse onward.

Her man had left in such haste that morning, riding straight across the road ahead. He had gradually disappeared into clouds of dust that turned into glittering mists in the sunlight. He had left as though he was headed for conquest, riding towards glory with black blazing eyes and lips drawn into a smile. Khalideh had watched him from the window bars, never moving her eyes away for hours after their goodbyes.

And her beloved did not return. There were those who tried in vain to convince her of her unfortunate fate and to reconcile her with her pain. But she refused to accept her misfortune and each day, fresh hope awakened in her heart; every day, she would await her husband's return, preparing at length and ever so sweetly to greet her beloved. There is the eyeshadow around her deep-set eyes; there, the pungent pomade of her hair; here are her delicate, flowing garments whose folds enveloped her supple, graceful movements and became an extension, almost a shadow, of herself; here is the sandalwood incense to scent her bath, and the henna to tint her fingernails with the red of quivering rose petals, to accentuate the fairness of her hands and bare arms, her milky smooth chest and swan-like neck, which lengthened and bloomed into the crowning beauty of her face.

All in vain… in vain… The departed beloved returns no more. Just as summer flowers wither in haste, his love had grown and blossomed, matured too soon and then wilted away. But Khalideh Hanum, who had fixed her beautiful, dreamy eyes to the desolate road, awaited her beloved with alarm, at first, and then, gradually, with sorrow; but her bold, noble love never once knew despair…

***

Months went by and then years. The released woman became an old lady, shriveled from her loneliness and anguish. But her persistent suffering kept her mighty heart young. Every day, she grooms herself with the same attention to detail. She wears her jewelry and prepares to greet her beloved. Her eyes are bleary from watching the road for his return; her skin is discolored and wrinkled, and her emaciated face bears the indelible stamp of a long-suffering woman. But she waits, surviving with her memories of the past, kindling her hopes with recollections of unforgettable moments, and gilding her old age with that fleeting, distant joy.

How they had loved each other then and how beautiful they had been in their love and tenderness! Their love ignited into a raging blaze, and its powerful thrust made them soar high above the earthly plane. As the earth throbs beneath the hooves of a swift stallion, so their breasts boomed with passion and ecstasy. They lived the rapture of a thousand lifetimes in a single kiss, so immense and formidable was their love.

Khalideh Hanum was as light and supple as a feather. And her youthful face radiated with the white of her skin and the black of her sparkling, uncomprehending eyes. At times, her gaze receded behind the veil of a dreamy gaze. But then, they would glow with the flame of an unquenchable fire that roared with bursts of joy. Her husband, a brave valiant soldier, whose feet seldom withdrew from their stirrups, had fallen captive to the wistful and mesmerizing beauty of those eyes.

For just one season, for one glorious sundrenched season, joy had reigned in their nest, until the petals of roses and jasmines that had budded too soon wilted and fell, taking the last of their perfume with them; and the verdant vines went pale as they lost their color in the sun.

***

Night has pressed on, and the autumn squalls have paved the sky with black clouds. Darkness is roaming, peering through the emptiness with its many eyes. There is a patch of cypresses, motionless and solemn, beside the quiet, now uninhabited house. In the family cemetery, their outline appears even blacker than night. Slender and dark they stand, waiting day after day for the wind to lend its breath and voice to their evergreen tips. The southerly wind rocks them gently in its big, warm currents, as their heady, pungent scent perfumes their bright surroundings. Intoxicated by their fragrance and perhaps also the pervading light, migrant black birds swoop madly through the air. Then they perch on their branches and listen to their melodic sobs.

The darkness is deep and still, and the cypresses are now shivering in the frigid wind. The melancholy murmur of their rustling leaves sends whispers through the family cemetery.

One day, perhaps, the long and desolate road will finally throb beneath the hooves of that same rider's steed. But the eyes that once watched and waited are now shut. A lantern flickers on a latticed tombstone. Take a moment to stop there, oh rider. As you charged carefree through your life, encountering new joys along the way, a heart awaited your return in vain behind the bars of a locked cage.

The night is dark, and the wind is blowing its icy breath through neighborhoods that remain as quiet and unknowable as a vast cemetery. Only the lantern on Khalideh Hanum's white tombstone continues to flicker with undying hope as it awaits her beloved's return. Because they are saintly, those who love and who wait. They can kindle their hopes even in the frozen ground of a graveyard.

The Death of a Child

For several days, a group of refugees from Rumelia had been temporarily sheltering in the courtyard of a beautiful grand mosque in Scutari. Unable to stay and dispersed among the fragments of their belongings, they were waiting impatiently to finally depart for the new designated settlement.

The majority were women. And from old to young, their pallid faces all bore the expression of a painful shock from which it seemed they would never recover. A series of horrific, devastating ordeals had turned them into the disfigured semblance of human beings. They were wrapped in tattered rags and veiled with strips of cloth. They had children of every age, all barely clothed, some covered with sores or dirt. The men were either elderly or infirm, and there were wounded deserters among them. Their extreme misery, both mental and physical, had forged them into a hideous mass, which consisted of every dreadful form representing the whole horror of the failed war.

Day in and day out, the long line of refugees would continue its journey along the main route. And the commotion of the departing crowds and the occasional lowing of their cattle, homesick and heartbreaking, would mingle with the persistent thunder of canons exploding in the distance.

Seated in a circle, the mournful refugee women would suddenly awaken to their painful memories and begin to wail, to curse, and to lament. Meanwhile, the children would gather around the many spouts of the *ubdesse** fountain, or in the shade of ancient mulberry and maple trees, pretending to be at war as they would relive the various episodes of catastrophic events. And then, absolute silence would reign. All of them, old and young, would become numb to the world, stiff and speechless from their pain, unaware that they were swaying to the persistent sound of thundering artillery.

---

*. Ablution. (Tr.)

***

The sunny noon sky shines bright. A quiver of intense light occasionally cuts through the diaphanous air and sparkles like a display of fireworks. Everything has turned into gold. The refugees' faded rags reflect what color they have left. The motionless trees look virtually transparent in the blanching light. Even the dust on the ground and the threads of swaying spiderwebs appear to be gilded. Great, immense, purifying, and venerable, the mosque's silhouette stands alongside the graceful curves of its grand domes in the glory of all this light and luminosity. Overhead, the sharp tips of the soaring minarets taper into imperceptible points blending into the radiant heavens.

Below, in the shade of the mosque, behind columns or beneath the small, graceful arch of the blue and gold-encrusted entrance dome, the refugees now occupy the places of common beggars, miserable from impatience and boredom. They are weary with anguish and have already reconciled with their misery as they discuss their plans to leave and begin a new life.

One young woman remains absent from those conversations and hopes. Withdrawn to one side, she is kneeling with a child in her lap. A white kerchief covers her head and a discolored rag is pulled across her mouth and the lower half of her face. But the eyes beneath her long lashes are moist as they ignite in her broad ashen face, achingly loving and replete with tormented tenderness. Every time she fixes her gaze upon her ailing child, those ever more anguished eyes blur in the surrounding light.

The little one screams and does not want to sleep, his shrill, broken screams of pain rise, fade, resume, and sometimes continue in distressed breaths. And with each shriek, his frail body writhes, his wrapped limbs twist, and his entire being quakes with screams of pain.

He is already a few months old, but every day, he weighs lighter in his mother's arms, and he has already assumed the horrifying appearance of a miscarried fetus. His forehead has become broader, and his skull has softened. Beneath the bindings on his forehead, his gaping, painfully stupefied eyes seem to occupy his entire face. And every time he opens his twisted mouth, one can see the fever-stricken child's already discolored gums and desiccated tongue quivering like a cord through his contorted lips.

The little one does not want to sleep, and he is beside himself, while his mother struggles to soothe him. She has heard that an epidemic which only afflicts children is sweeping through the refugees, and she thinks anxiously of her child. She has heard that some mothers abandoned their dying children so that they could join the departing groups. And that there were some who, at every stop on that horrific journey, had left their loved ones behind so that they could move on, each time fewer in numbers.

The sun dazzles the unfortunate woman's eyes, and the magnificent, luminous beauty of her surroundings feels cruel and hostile to her, alien to her anguish. She does not know how she feels, but incoherent imprecations rise to her lips, while she continues to kneel, holding the little one close to her breast and struggling to console him. The closeness of his mother's breast and her rocking arms momentarily silence the infant, but his pain reawakens and seizes his whole fragile being. The ailing child opens his eyes, his pupils dilated, and lets out a long lingering shriek that leaves him breathless.

No one wants to go to their aid. Their hearts have turned to stone after all those horrible incidents and nightmarish events. The old women sometimes turn to her with heavy hearts and frowning looks, blaming her for sparing him her milk, although she is relentless in stubbornly pushing her nipple into the infant's mouth, trying to silence that heartbreaking voice. But her milk spills out of the child's twisted blue lips and dries there.

What sort of pain had settled into that tender life? His smile had never bloomed, withering on his face before it could. His eyes had scarcely begun to recognize his mother's features, when suddenly clouds of pain had shrouded them in darkness. He had only just discerned the moving trees with their swaying shadows; he had only just noticed the sun's bright rays, and his cries of joy had scarcely echoed the countless sounds of nature, disrupting moments of long pensive silence, as he had watched the changing shapes that adult eyes failed to see.

The world, a dark chaos, was just emerging from its mists, was just revealing itself to his senses, was just assuming shape and color and giving form to its fantastical and exquisite displays, when suddenly, the pain rose like a wave and seized his entire being within itself, drowning his mind and the fragile, unformed, and disconnected islands of his senses. And everything descends once again into darkness and unknowing, and the life in that fragile body now flickers like a flame that will soon be extinguished.

***

It is evening now. The setting sun's last rays pierce the gray mists shrouding the horizon and paint it with shades of red. Radiant clouds the color of black cherry gently transform, while streaks of light in the gilded firmament appear to hover in midair and point towards vast distances leading onto strange worlds. The evening light ripples with puffs of pink and red, and the mosque glows. Its glass, metal and porcelain surfaces reflect the whole spectrum of colors in the last rays of light.

A final glimmer of sunshine falls upon the dying child's expression, illuminating it without penetrating his frigid face and his dazed gaping eyes with its light and warmth.

The refugees have prepared their bundles and are sitting in a circle beside their belongings. An order has arrived, and they will leave the following morning. Before the mosque shuts its doors, the old men and the infirm come leaning on their canes to join them. And turning their brows westward, their fingers stroking their prayer beads, they sit in silent contemplation. The blasts – some deep, some shrill – of the departing ships' horns tear through the silence, their echoes reverberating and eventually fading away. The commotion in the nearby market and the clatter of passing carts upset them. They are startled. And memories of the catastrophe stab through their pain-numbed brains. An old woman invokes her murdered child, "*Oghlooooom...Oghlooooom!*"

***

The young woman gazes with painful astonishment upon the sundrenched face of her dying child. The little one is no longer screaming. His lips are twisting, his face contorting, exhibiting all the expressions of a scream, but his voice remains stifled. And these mute expressions of suffering assume a monstrous dimension in the sun's final rays, which ignite into a mask of sparkling light on the face of the dying child.

He was his mother's first. And he had arrived into this world over there, in that distant little village, on a beautiful warm spring evening. They had celebrated his arrival like a victory, because his father had been blessed with a son.

Where is his father…? Where were those moments of joy…? The image of a serene, flat landscape suddenly rises before her. Fruiting trees stemming from the rough stretches of freshly ploughed earth stand tall, extending their shadows throughout the sun-soaked orchards. Flocks of oxen and sheep emerge from the deep blue of the distant horizon, creating moving blotches of white as they disperse… Gray and white clouds speed across the sky, shading the village rooftops, where the wispy tips of smoking chimneys rise steadily into the air.

The young woman wants to fix her eyes upon that happy former life, but saturated with tears, they meet her infant's gaze, which no longer holds the expression of a child, but rather of a worldly, long-suffering man. In those few moments of excruciating pain, he has lived through every stage of human suffering. The little one now possesses the furrowed, wrinkled face of an old woman, where his eyes express shock, fury, outrage, and most of all, bewilderment as they fix upon uncanny, incomprehensible images, until, exhausted, they acquiesce and fade beneath his eyelids…

The sun shone one last time and disappeared. A corridor of light stole away, shooting through the sky as the heavy shadows of night emerged quietly from this earth. Deep inside the strange city, darker, more obscure shadows suddenly appear, passing through like enormous trembling specters. One by one, the women gather, congregating around the mourning mother and attempt to console her. Their departure had been set for tomorrow, and if the child's death had been prolonged, his mother would have been forced to stay behind or to desert her helpless son, because it would have been impossible to bring him along, when transporting the sick to the new settlements was strictly forbidden. And so, it was God's assistance and command that had saved both her and her innocent son, God rest his soul…

But the inconsolable mother wept and grieved all through the night, refusing to sleep or at least to rest. Sitting apart from her companions of misery, she wept with tragic screams that tore through the night. Her eyes were fixed to the European shore, which glistened with countless lights and seemed to be submerged in peaceful indifference, as the muffled blasts of thundering artillery continued to unsettle their world.

On the Threshold: Scenes from Life in Turkey

Feyzi Bey slowed his pace when he, at last, saw a passerby on the dusty, desolate thoroughfare. He was approaching him from ahead, carrying an uprooted sapling on one shoulder and a shovel in his other hand.

When he was close enough, Feyzi Bey greeted him with a salute, "Brotherhood!"

"Brotherhood!" replied the peasant and stopped.

Feyzi Bey then took the opportunity to ask for the whereabouts of his friend's, Nahad's, residence.

The peasant became suspicious but feigned indifference. He pulled his red handkerchief out of his pocket and, as he wiped his forehead and cheeks, he examined Feyzi Bey with a few sidelong glances.

"You're looking for our residence," he finally said with a smile and asked that his guest follow him.

Feyzi and Nahad were old friends. They had become close when they were still only adolescents. And their friendship had grown to be one of shared ideals. A decade earlier, Feyzi had left Istanbul to study in Paris, but after graduation, he had been compelled to remain abroad, at his father's urging. Because back then, being young and a university student were considered crimes in themselves. Nahad had stayed in Turkey, but the two friends had maintained their close ties through a clandestine correspondence. In those long years of their morose, hopeless youth, with one confined inside his own country and the other in exile abroad, they had just one source of consolation. Those were their long letters to each other, where they relayed their dreams and various plans for the rebirth of their unfortunate country. But eventually all the forces on which they had laid their hopes had been crushed. During the dying years of the tyrannical government, all the young men in their circle of acquaintances had either disarmed and assumed government positions or they had disappeared and been driven to the pits of Anatolia.

Feyzi Bey had not lost hope, however, and he had attempted for over a year to reenter the country, so that he could collaborate with the organizations that wanted to stage an uprising against the tyrannical regime.

But when he had enthusiastically sent his friend a letter a few months earlier, hoping that they would work together, he had received a disturbing reply that had driven him to uncertainty. Was it possible that his faithful comrade, the leonine Nahad, had, in his turn, lost his moral strength? Feyzi did not even want to imagine such an eventuality. But how else could one make sense of Nahad's stated skepticism towards the growing movement, and especially his aversion to the promises of collaboration made by some of the civilized countries to the revolutionary Turks, provided that they succeeded in fomenting a nationwide movement to topple the tyrannical government?

Knowing that he would soon reenter the country, Feyzi Bey did not respond to his friend's letter. And now, as he went over his objections in his mind, he worried about one thing: how would he find Nahad? He recalled his honest face, his somewhat rough demeanor, but also his modest, unaffected spirit. The brilliant serenity of his powerful, sincere disposition radiated from his grayish eyes. Could it be that those eyes were dimmed by vice?

Walking with the peasant in silence, Feyzi Bey subtly made some inquiries.

"So, did Nahad Bey cross over to the Asian side a little while ago?"

"After his father died, our Bey came to Libade with his sister and is now working in agriculture. I'm employed in his service."

"Was it his land or did he purchase it?"

"He inherited it from his mother, but it was in neglect. Nahad Bey prefers to keep to himself in these difficult times."

Frightened by his own words, the peasant looked around warily, then sighed and kept his peace.

Summer was approaching its end, and nature had assumed the delicate hue of fading colors and waning light. One could make out the distant hills through the white mists. Clouds rolled by and ignited the sky now and then. Their shifting shapes and colors seemed to permeate the surrounding world.

The peasant paused and extended his arm eastward. Red-tiled roofs appeared through hazy, shimmering ripples. Behind them rose the spikey silhouette of a cypress tree. The delicate fragrances of cut grass and hay wafted from the harvests of nearby fields, and the air was buzzing with the frenzied dance of countless beetles, their gilded bodies sparkling in the light.

Water gurgled in the distance.

"It was quite a long walk up the hill," muttered Feyzi and thanked the peasant. "I took you out of your way, I hope you can forgive me… I'm no stranger. Nahad and I were friends from school."

The peasant's furrowed face smoothed. His small, piercing eyes smiled. He waved goodbye and took leave.

Left alone, Feyzi was gripped once again by melancholy. Mother nature's serenity clashed with the conflict in his soul and tormented him. How was he going to find his old friend, Nahad? The despotic tyranny had seemed to quietly suck the blood even out of those who had once been heroic and fearless. A heavy veil of hopeless grief had shrouded the whole country. All voices had been drowned, and all eyes were now bereft of their light.

The air echoed with the long, mournful lows of cattle disturbed by mosquitoes in the nearby pastures, and then stillness reigned once more.

Feyzi Bey regained his composure and headed toward the red tiles.

***

Feyzi walked along a path extending through the cultivated fields and aimed for a house surrounded by a garden fence. The gate was open, so he went in. A guard dog barked, and one could hear the monotonous creaking pump of an artesian well in the distance. There was an old woman reclining on a mat under a maple tree, leaning her elbow on the ground, and resting her head in her hand. A white, youthful silhouette passed between a row of trees like a shadow.

"Safiyeh," yelled the old woman as she raised her head, "call your brother, there's someone at the door."

And then she lifted the veil from her shoulders to her head, got to her feet, and went into the house.

"Safiyeh," sounded a male voice, "where is Jemal?"

Feyzi Bey hesitated. The white silhouette appeared once more, approached him, and shading her forehead with a hand, looked up at him. Behind the girl, a brawny young man, wearing a simple shirt and a pair of gray trousers, walked towards him.

"Nahad," cried Feyzi, his voice choking.

"Feyzi, my dearest friend!"

The bygone years had altered them both, but they recognized each other and embraced with brotherly affection.

"Let's go into the house."

"No, I prefer to stay here… on the straw mat…"

"Feyzi, so here we are…"

"Nahad, you know something?… I've been looking for you for over a week. I couldn't even imagine that you… you hadn't written to me about this."

"I didn't write… it was a personal matter. For one thing, I was forced to make this choice… Life there was suffocating me, but I'm quite content now. We're isolated here, but we're free. I've been waiting for you for days, Feyzi… When I heard that you were returning to Istanbul, I was both overjoyed and depressed."

Nahad's sunburnt face wrinkled. His grayish eyes darkened, and he knitted his brows. He pointed vaguely in the direction of the distant city and muttered, "So, you ended up in that hellhole too."

Feyzi Bey gently shook his head.

"You must fight and win," he said as he held back his voice.

Nahad watched his friend with admiration.

Feyzi Bey was a slight young man of average height. The red of his fez and the chestnut hair showing on his forehead made his dark complexion and the taut skin of his slightly prominent cheekbones appear almost dull. The full lips swelling beneath his delicate mustache expressed disdain. A firm chin accentuated his stern expression, but he had beautiful black eyes below long eyebrows that gazed back with such a dreamy, indefinably sad expression.

"I'm a full-blown peasant now," said Nahad, embarrassed suddenly by his muddy hands. Nahad took a few steps back and called out, "Safiyeh!… where have you disappeared to?"

A female voice could be heard nearby, and Safiyeh appeared.

She was a dusky young woman, no more than twenty years old, wearing a white *entari* gathered at the waist with a belt. She blushed as she approached her brother, but, at the same time, she could not help turning her smiling, curious eyes towards the guest. Her arched brows, which were conjoined with a downy fuzz, gave her lovely face a haughty expression. A white veil hardly covered her tilting head, and one of her fingertips played with a black lock of hair that had fallen over her cheek. The yellow amber necklace on her bare neck inclined toward her tilted head.

"Safiyeh, let me introduce you to my dearest friend, Feyzi Bey, whom I've often mentioned to you."

Safiyeh took a step forward and then shied away, because Feyzi Bey had fixed his eyes stubbornly to the ground and seemed to be unwell. At that moment, the young man was furious with himself for the incorrigible timidity that had suddenly overcome him. He was amazed by Nahad's ease and his show of trust, as though he had conquered an emotion that was unconquerable. But his fear of betraying that trust made him apprehensive, and he did not want to raise his eyes up to the exposed face of Nahad's sister. To him, Safiyeh was veiled.

Sensing his friend's discomfort, Nahad smiled and kindly led his sister away.

"Safiyeh!... come draw some water so I can wash my hands."

***

Sitting cross-legged on the straw mat, the two friends were engaged in intense conversation. When Safiyeh returned to the garden with her elderly aunt, Feyzi was transformed. He no longer noticed the women's presence, and he continued to speak in the same abrupt, almost offensive tone.

"We must destroy everything from the bottom up. We must not only topple this vile regime, at all costs, but also to declare war against the past, war, irreconcilable war."

Nahad listened quietly and pensively to his friend's rage-filled voice.

"We must destroy everything and erect something new," continued Feyzi almost in a state of intoxication... "We must employ the swiftest, the most direct course of action possible."

The blood throbbed in his temples, and his eyes blurred at the sight of the peaceful, sunny bucolic scene. The anger directed at himself had not abated, and he seemed to be struggling hopelessly to smash the shackles of his own making, having felt their chafing weight upon him moments earlier. Those arched brows conjoined by a downy fuzz seemed to be mocking his impotence. He made every effort to contain himself, but his mind shot past his intentions. His soul seemed to be sprinting ahead of him to hasten his approach towards the barely perceptible future. Nahad's thoughtful expression drove him to distraction. He suddenly felt prepared to undertake any sacrifice, and a surge of pride rose in his agitated soul.

He watched the two women retreating with slow steps. The sun was setting over the horizon. The surrounding scenery darkened from the looming shadow of a gloomy cloud.

"We've done enough dreaming, planning, and thinking," Feyzi said with despairing intensity. "We now have to get to work and I'm certain, Nahad, that I will have you as a brother in arms."

Nahad gestured to gently decline.

Feyzi failed to grasp the meaning of that gesture, and added sullenly, "What's the point of preserving our pointless lives? We were born as slaves, we've lived as slaves, let's at least die as free men."

Nahad was about to speak when Safiyeh came out holding a tray. Her tiny red moccasins squeaked slightly on the straw mat. Her supple figure stooped and turned to the side as she presented the tray. With trembling hands, Feyzi Bey took the cup of *kahveh* and placed it on the ground.

Still standing, Safiyeh watched him. A mighty expression of such powerful and violent intensity radiated from the young Turk's whole being that it made her quake with awe. Beneath his fused, frowning brows, his eyes had lost their sadness and burned with passion. Feyzi felt the warmth of the young woman's gaze and raised his head. The arched brows rose on her smooth face, and Safiyeh's wide eyes confronted the young man's look. At that moment, Feyzi blushed, as though he were seeing her for the first time. And bearing the impact of her beauty and elegance with all the might that his being could muster, he gazed at length and trembled.

***

"If successful, a revolution led by a few people is an attack on the government, and, if unsuccessful, it's an insurgency. To achieve anything fundamental and lasting, we must exhort the people. They're the only ones who can enact a real revolution."

Feyzi Bey heard his friend's words, but he could no longer follow the conversation. It was as though the harmony between his intentions and his decisions had been broken. His eyes had lost their sternness and wandered gently over random objects until they met those of Safiyeh, who kept moving around nervously at the back of the garden.

"I am an Anatolian, and a Turk born of Turks," continued Nahad. "Why would I want to compromise my mindset and lifestyle to accommodate hostile, alien ideas? If we really want to rise up, we must join the people. We must rouse them from their listless lives. At the moment, it is a paralyzed body that is slowing our advance. I had given that a lot of thought when I wrote you this letter. It's not the empire that we have to save, it's our people."

"No, no, I disagree," thought Feyzi, but his objections vanished. Because, at that moment, he was worried about what Safiyeh had thought of him earlier, when he could not bring himself to look at her and greet her like any other civilized man. That is what it will be like with emancipated Turkish women, he was thinking as he kept his eyes on Safiyeh and watched her agile movements with wonderment, as though dream had become reality before his very eyes.

He suddenly came back to his senses and told his friend, "Where is that people?"

"We'll find our true people where they are, in their native lands, not over there."

Nahad's hand aimed at distant, inimical Istanbul.

Feyzi lost his composure and replied with bitter derision, "Just because you've crossed over to the Asian side, you think your issue has been resolved."

In fact, for an instant, the prospect of a people that had mastered its own fate also rose before Feyzi Bey. But that seemed to be a distant, obscure goal. More than ever, what he wanted was the glory of a fight. To die if necessary, but to do his part. He had an insatiable appetite for leaping into action, and all else amounted to anxiety and the mindless prolongation of cruel times.

"No," replied Nahad in earnest. "I know full well that my issue has not been resolved. It's all still nothing but confusion and uncertainty. Here, it's true, I'm not in the very heart of the people, but I'm on the threshold of our native country. I may not succeed in drawing up a plan of action, but there will be others who will come after us and perceive things more clearly. It's the Turkish people that will save Turkey; not me, and not you."

"Nahad, don't you think that this will divide our paths," shouted Feyzi in exasperation.

Nahad remained pensive for a moment, but instantly shook his head to say no.

"We will soon unite on a much bigger path."

***

Feyzi stood up and prepared to leave. He thought of inviting Nahad to his sister's house in Istanbul, but he hesitated. His thoughts scattered momentarily, and his eyes surveyed the back of the garden. Then he immediately thought of staying for a few days on the Asian shore, Beylerbey, where he had an elderly uncle, and he happily relayed the decision to his friend.

"I'll be an Anatolian for a few days too, Nahad. I'll stay at my uncle's house, near Scutari. We can meet more often that way."

"Feyzi, my brother," said Nahad enthusiastically, "you'll see for yourself that we're modest folk. Come round to our place whenever you can, and we'll talk, we'll talk plenty."

"You have a stunningly beautiful garden," said Feyzi as he wiped his forehead.

He could not make sense of his own turmoil. He kept dillydallying, and his lips trembled with emotion.

"Let's go to the rose garden. My sister, Safiyeh, tends to the roses herself," said Nahad.

They walked together through the flower beds and stopped in front of a fence. Leaning over a rosebush, Safiyeh was pruning the stems. She straightened herself and turned her smiling eyes to her only brother's only guest.

"It's a marvel, not a garden," Feyzi told Safiyeh, who was approaching them, tentatively.

"It was too hot this year," said Safiyeh in her sweet, frank voice. "Some of the bushes would have bloomed again, but they didn't bud… if only it had rained a little more…"

As she spoke, she bent over a rosebush and plucked a red rose, which she presented to Feyzi Bey.

Their fingers touched upon the thorny stem, and they smiled to each other like intimate old friends.

***

The family home of Feyzi Bey's uncle was a wooden structure. There was such perfect silence behind those closed, caged windows that it was impossible to discern whether anyone had ever lived there or indeed continued to live there. Nevertheless, he had a large family. His old uncle's elderly wife and her daughters-in-law remained confined to their quarters, while Saduk Bey wandered aimlessly, pottered about in the garden, constantly did the upkeep on the run-down parts of the house, and spent the rest of his time sitting by the door, in front of the garden, where the basil wilted from the heat, drooping to the ground, and the seasonal flowers slowly withered in the sun. When the muezzin sang the evening prayer from the minaret, Saduk Bey, wrapped in his proverbial robe, would take his time quietly performing the namaz after his afternoon nap. Then, he would retreat to the garden that he tended and he would have a cup of *kahveh* and smoke his nargileh. The *nefair** who had been placed in his service some time ago had voluntarily decided to remain and continued to serve him loyally and without complaint.

---

*. Private soldier. (Tr.)

Saduk Bey was active and restless by nature, and he was unbearably bored by this idle life. But he was incapable of initiating any kind of work or hobby for himself. In the winter, he complained that the days were too short, and that evening sets before dawn, so that he cannot devote himself to any serious work. And in the summer, he complained about the long days, when his boredom prevailed not only over him, but also over the entire household. The more bored he grew and the more acutely he felt the weight of all the empty passing time, the more idle he became, and his gray, vacuous existence became occupied with frivolous cares, meaningless and non-existent threats.

One of Saduk Bey's primary distractions was to berate his *nefair* by finding all manner of shortcomings in his service, showing him how to clean the courtyard, how to position the armchair, how to replenish his nargileh, kindling its little flames, cleaning and polishing its metal parts. And as the *nefair* would stand to attention and heed his master without a peep, his temper would rage.

"You Anatolian hick... why don't you say something? Answer me! You keep standing there, dumb as a rock, to defy me!" But when the *nefair* would venture to make the slightest move just to open his mouth, Saduk Bey's fury would climax at the very first syllable.

"You son of a bitch, how dare you, you, you!... talk back to me... get out of my sight, don't you dare show your face again!"

And as soon as the servant would disappear, Saduk Bey would shout, "Ahmed, I'll have your head, Ahmed, get over here and take my orders!"

Regardless, master and servant had a contented relationship and could not seem to part ways. When the entire household would explode with the former soldier's swearing and shouting, the servant would think, "He must love me a lot. If my master didn't love me like one of his own children, why would he go through all this trouble and give me instructions on how to do everything?"

He would have preferred it if the old man followed through with his gesticulated threats, if he stood up, attacked him, and beat him. Ahmed believed that must be his master's ultimate expression of love, and when he received those blows without complaint, he would demonstrate his endless loyalty and self-sacrifice.

And Saduk Bey was pleased with the fact that he could find a reason to raise his voice. As his roars bellowed in the marble courtyard, he would take pleasure in hearing their echoes. He found the sound of his own voice intoxicating, maddeningly thrilling, because it would remind him of a time when he enjoyed active employment and glory. But those memories would instantly turn bitter, because they would remind him of his misfortunes. Why had they made him retire early? Wasn't it thanks to his *zalim*[*] brother?... oooh... ooooh...

"Who did you think you were? Did you actually believe that you could defy an order from the top?... What were you setting your hopes on, you imbecile?!"

He searched his thoughts to see whether there had been anyone on this earth who had done anything as stupid as his brother.

"He did it to himself, he did it to me, he did it to my children... he took his whole family down with him, for shame, for shame."

One of Saduk Bey's sons was born a dimwit, but they had married him off some time earlier and managed to find him a job. He had a fleshy, pallid, fat, flabby face. And he behaved like an automaton, unreceptive to his family and to his time, exempt from and devoid of all cares.

His second son resembled his father and had the same restless disposition. But he had not been able to hold on to any job. Great pains were taken on three separate occasions to place him, but he was dismissed from the third arrangement.

Saduk Bey sometimes ascribed his son's failures to his brother's actions, which put a stain on the entire family, made them *mimlemish*,[†] and at other times, he placed the blame on his son's rebellious, impudent nature.

"Before you can straighten up, you need to learn how to bow down, *oghloom!*... If you don't break your back when you're young, you'll have to do it when you go gray, and you'll be miserable, no one will show you any respect."

---

[*]. Tough-guy. (Tr.)
[†]. Marked. (Tr.)

But, at the sight of his son's cynical smirk and restlessness, Saduk Bey raised a lament, "Oh, those were the days. Our time has come and gone. The winds of madness are blowing among the youth of today."

But Saduk Bey's primary and unyielding worry concerned something else. Ten years prior, the Minister of War had unexpectedly called him in and buried him in a series of incomprehensible but harsh reprimands. Then, he had informed him that, in light of his old age and his years of service until now, "*effendimiz*"* has decided to show mercy by sparing him his punishment. But he was being dismissed from active duty and could now consider himself retired.

Shaken, trembling, and stupefied by a terror like no other, he stood there gaping. Sweat dripped from his temples and brow. He had lost all sense of reality and had no memory of being escorted out. These were evil times. Even prominent men could be dismissed and disappeared from one day to the next just for uttering a "yes" or a "no." What had he possibly said or done? Saduk Bey came to his senses outside in the fresh air. Riding a closed carriage on his way down from Babuh Ali, disgraced and reproached, he found his resolve for a moment and considered the possibility of lodging a complaint, objecting, demanding an explanation. The soldier suddenly felt valor and pride awaken in his soul.

"All I have is a soul, that is all they can take away from me," he thought indignantly. "I should have said this... I should have replied like that ..."

He reminded himself that he was a military man and that he had chosen his profession with a readiness to sacrifice his life at any given moment. Why should he be afraid? From what? Is death on the battlefield the only worthwhile death? Hadn't his time come to show his courage and worth?

These beautiful sentiments lasted until they reached the bridge. When he arrived in Beylerbey, he learned that the tragedy that had befallen him was the result of his brother's – Feyzi's father – insubordination. He had refused to take command of a repressive regiment that was being sent to Rumelia on orders to use the most brutal measures necessary to suppress a local uprising. He also learned that his

---

*. Meaning, "our effendi." (Tr.) The Sultan. (Au.)

brother had been condemned to exile and that there was no knowing what other disasters might befall his family.

The possibility of those unspecified misfortunes extinguished and destroyed every semblance of psychological resilience left in that old soldier. From morning to night, he lived with the foreboding of someone awaiting some awful news. Terror crept into his soul like a mist, shrouding his feelings and thoughts, stifling his pride and valor, and eventually dominating his whole life. His words and actions became timid and apprehensive. All his friends and acquaintances abandoned him. And he withdrew into a solitary life at home, where his wife and daughters provoked his terror by sustaining it with all the pieces of cryptic news that they received from the outside world.

It was not until many years later, when the anticipated tragedy had not eventuated after all, that Saduk Bey was finally convinced that all was forgotten. And he relaxed into a degree of calm. But that insidious terror awaited him in the pits of his soul. And it could awaken at any moment to overtake him with all its might.

***

The day had advanced to a late hour, and the elderly soldier, weary from idleness and fatigue, had retreated to his wife's room, which was located on the first floor of the house. The caged windows darkened the room, because the upper branches of the cedar just outside the house blocked the final rays of twilight. Their two daughters, who were still of a tender age, were serving them. And their daughter-in-law was preparing some snacks on a tray, because Saduk Bey had a habit of drinking one or two glasses of *oghi*[*] before dinner.

It was at that moment that they pounded on the door. The two young men had entered the house. And that surprise visit filled the householders with fright and alarm.

Saduk Bey stood up, and in a rush to preempt the presumed danger, he headed for the courtyard, where he came face to face with Feyzi Bey.

"*Amooja*,[†] it's me, Feyzi!..."

---

[*]. Aniseed liqueur. (Tr.)
[†]. Uncle. (Tr.)

Feyzi bent down to kiss his uncle's hand, which felt cadaverously stiff and cold to the touch.

"Is that you, Feyzi, *oghloom*?" muttered the old man, his voice quavering.

He hesitated, while his evasive gaze avoided the young man.

"Your arrival is most welcome," he finally willed himself to say, "right this way, let's go to my room."

Despite his uncle's politesse, Feyzi Bey felt the chill of his tentatively spoken words. When they climbed the stairs up to the straw matted room, Saduk Bey went over and sat on his knees in one corner of the cushions extending along the window, and he immediately called his nephew over to him. Trembling, he took his long string of beads out of his pocket and informed Feyzi that he had not been apprised of his arrival and that his surprise visit had given him a fright.

Feyzi watched his uncle without uttering a word. Despite the extreme heat, Saduk Bey was wearing a heavy *hurha*,[*] out of which jutted his skinny neck and dusky arms. He also had a sallow face that looked almost desiccated, as though it had been scorched by an inner inferno. And the white cap on his bald head conformed to the shape of his Turanian skull, accentuating all its peculiar features. A white beard wreathed his face, and his protruding cheekbones emphasized the equally protuberant line of his arching brows. His eye sockets looked like cavities containing the faint glimmer of black pupils. Dazed and terrified, they belonged to a restless man, who believed that he was perpetually under threat.

Suddenly, Feyzi felt that he was a stranger in that house, and that an unbreachable gulf gaped between him and his most intimates. With this terrible realization, he recalled Libade's peaceful idyll, his friend's welcoming treatment, "despite the fact that our paths have diverged," he thought sullenly.

Saduk Bey was still quiet when his eldest, Nazmi, entered the room. Slim, graceful, and well-groomed, he had his father's overall bearing, but without the same withered appearance. At first, Nazmi entered

---

[*]. An oriental-style robe. (Tr.)

hesitantly, but his heart seemed to open as he approached his relative, and they began to converse. Every time the conversation would assume a critical tone regarding current events and people, the old man would show signs of unease and grumble. Rattling the beads in his hand, his lips would quickly repeat the Prophet's attributes, "The greatest, the most merciful, the mightiest..."

Nazmi listened to his cousin intently and with great interest as he spoke of Europe. He was parched for liberal ideas, and he had an insatiable yearning to know and experience that distant, utopian life, which was called a civilized existence. Up until then, he thought that he had incorporated a European style into his dress and demeanor, and he was prepared to blindly accept anything that was from Europe – ideas, lifestyles, furnishings, clothing. But his mentality remained thoroughly Turkish, and those external elements accessorized his mindset without actually transforming it. He was naturally gifted with many virtues. He was brave and proud and was loath to bow his head to anyone. Bred in a military family, he had an excessively acute sense of honor. And for that reason, he had been unable to retain his post in politics.

At dinnertime, the old man's dimwitted son also joined them, and as they sat on little stools around a large, round tray, the men of the family took their meals in an oriental manner. After dinner, the old man went to sleep, and that is when Feyzi Bey ventured to ask after his uncle's daughters and their mother.

***

Saliheh Hanum was raised in a modest family, and it was on account of her beauty that she had become Saduk Bey's wife. Now she was an old woman, but her face preserved some traces of her former beauty, although her body had been deformed by extreme obesity. She had been kind and affable by nature, but she had spoiled her character through her constant preoccupation with preserving the high social standing to which she had later attained. In her glory days, she had even stooped to using a tone of imperious condescension with her husband's inferiors. Uneducated and superstitious, she was barely willing to attend to her children's physical needs during her long days and years of idleness. Her favorite child was the dimwit, whose unintelligent face she deemed handsome, and whose lack of any will she interpreted as the expression of a good disposition. As a child, he had been his mother's plaything, and he was later treated as a clown by his sisters. His mother and sisters would giggle and delight in startling and confusing him by making him do ridiculous things. And after having a good laugh and amusing themselves to their hearts' content, their conscience would get the better of them, and they would shower him with love and tenderness as they called him names that were meant for puppies and other little pets.

Saduk Bey and Nazmi were not interested in the harem's goings-on, and over the years, the family members not only failed to forge new bonds, but on the contrary, even their natural bonds loosened, becoming severed.

Nazmi's two sisters – one aged twenty, and the other, eighteen – had grown in that environment. Like their mother, they were uneducated, even illiterate. Day after day, they tired of boredom and expended all their efforts on "passing the time." They were most content when the time would pass effortlessly. In the morning, they pined for the evening to come, and in the evening, they yearned for the day after.

"Oh no, it's still only seven," they used to complain on long summer days with the full force of their boredom and weariness.

Why were they in such a rush? What were their aims? Nothing. The future was a mist of uncertainty for them, and, in fact, even the vague outlines of an aspiration or a goal did not occur to them. They spent their long, unoccupied hours playing solitaire, gossiping about neighbors, tormenting their adolescent maid, entertaining themselves with their dimwitted brother, anxiously awaiting the arrival of gypsy fortunetellers, or they would take their time slowly nibbling on pieces of dried fruits and even watermelon seeds.

It was a great event when a *goriji*[*] would drop by to discuss some prospective grooms. Then, the hearts of these two young women would blossom with dreams, with delightful and hitherto unknown fantasies. But these were rare occasions. Behind the caged windows, amid all the countless emptied coffee cups and the incessant smoking, life passed by without leaving a trace.

---

*. A matchmaking woman. (Au.)

The entrance of a bride into that home was a momentous new event.

Their mother was intent on marrying off Hasan, and based on her specifications, they had located a few *goriji* women to find a gem that they deemed worthy of Saduk Bey's dimwitted son. Halideh was barely twenty years old, a slim, agile, sweet girl. A dream flickered in her moist, black eyes. She had resigned herself to her fate after meeting her husband, perhaps because she had no idea that there could be an alternative to her situation. Being an orphan, she had no family of her own, no one was concerned with her, and her resignation was also compelled by her life's circumstances.

She had attended school and received a rudimentary education. Whenever she could get her hands on her brother-in-law's books or newspapers, she would withdraw somewhere alone and read them. Her sisters-in-law's uneducated, uncultivated situation surprised and distressed her, but she had no idea how best to prevail upon them. If they had asked her to teach them how to read, she would have poured her whole heart into it, but they were too far removed from those sorts of concerns.

The attitude of the soldier's two daughters toward their sister-in-law was generally lukewarm. But they imposed their coarseness on Halideh, whom they subjected to their authority. Perhaps that was the very reason that she was unhappy, heartbroken, and melancholy, as though her innermost feelings had been deeply wounded. But Halideh's unhappiness, as well as her aspirations and troubles remained imperceptible. Her soul and mind were graced with tremendous talents, but her life lacked the sunlight that they needed to bloom. Along with the others, she too suffered from pathological boredom, but her idleness was replete with anguish. She used to occupy her long, empty hours by embroidering their veils. Leaning over the loom, as her fingers embroidered colorful imaginary flowers on the white muslin, her soul would wander through strange, distant realms. She felt urged and ready with her whole being to... to what? ... Nothing, she herself did not know.

When the *gorijis* would come for her sisters-in-law, praising their prospective grooms, Halideh would feel as flustered as though she was the intended bride, and she would make a mental note of her own favorites. She knew by instinct that her life had not yet begun and that her heart remained receptive to unknown feelings.

Her brother-in-law, Nazmi, was a figure of much interest for her, although they complained to no end about him. His mother, in particular, lamented her misfortune for giving birth to a child like that. And sometimes they discussed him with a sort of mysterious dread. Halideh had very few occasions to see Nazmi. He disdained his sisters and seldom visited the harem to see his mother. Halideh would rush to lift her veil from her shoulders and to cover her head, but her eyes would fix on him. She especially liked the masculine, authoritative tone of his voice.

Over time, Halideh discerned why the family thought of Nazmi as troublesome, and she instantly took his side. Although she had never had the occasion to discuss such matters with her brother-in-law, at heart, she was nonetheless in total agreement with his revolutionary ideals. Unable to determine the reasons, Halideh sensed that she was suffering, and what she held responsible was the prison that was confining her body and soul.

One day, she chanced upon a foreign source among Nazmi's newspapers. She devoured it. The source of her own suffering was illuminated. All at once, she learned that she was not alone in her misery, but that there are hundreds, thousands like her. New horizons opened before her, but the more hopes of liberation stirred within her, the more unbearable and oppressive became the prison in which she was a captive.

Noticing the disappearance of the prohibited newspaper, Nazmi ran to his mother, enraged, and heaped the blame on his sisters, who were entirely unaware of everything. Beside himself and terrified by the situation – because if that paper came out into the open, it could spell the end of him, because there were spies everywhere, even in one's own home – Nazmi returned to his room. Following behind him and risking the worst punishments, Halideh spoke timidly, "*Aghabey,*[*] I have the paper you lost."

---

*. Big brother. (Tr.)

Halideh pulled out the paper that she had kept over her breast beneath her veil and handed it to her brother-in-law.

"Halideh, Halideh!" said Nazmi, bewildered by the fire in the young woman's eyes.

"I won't tell anyone. I want you to give me more of them. I want to read them."

"Halideh!... my sister…"

They exchanged a long, heartfelt look. After that, on his saddest, most distressing days, when his mother, father, and sisters were unable to comprehend his pain, Nazmi would find contentment and consolation at the sight of Halideh raising her deep, sweet eyes to him from beneath her veil.

***

Feyzi Bey listened to Nazmi into the late hours of the night. Having finally found an outlet, the latter spoke of his family, his surroundings, and, of the prevailing circumstances. It was past midnight when they went to bed. But Feyzi Bey could not get to sleep. His thoughts were revisited by Nazmi's words, and he felt revulsion and rage as he pictured his cousin's life. His outrage grew so intense that he could not remain lying down. He also recalled Nahad's words, and he weighed them with a greater sense of clarity. But he was a jumble of emotions. Fierce hatred and rays of hope crisscrossed each other, turning his thoughts into chaos. He felt besieged by intangible folds of darkness that surged on all sides and began to drown him.

He got to his feet, opened the window, and looked outside. The house stood on a hill, and all of Beylerbey stretched before him, its caged houses shaded here and there by the canopies of ancient cedars. Across the way was the sea, glistening, dark blue. On the shore rose the royal palace with its lacework of engravings, and beyond the sea sprawled the edge of Europe, ethereal in the night, where a smattering of lights glittered in the hazy mist.

The summer night's still air possessed such clarity that one could even hear the murmuring shore. The ground exhaled a fog of steam that wafted low and rose no further. Lights burnt bright in the firmament. An odd buzzing broke away from the silence of inanimate objects and sent whispers through the air. It was as though the whole land had filled his ear with a murmured dream of joy and misery.

Suddenly, amid his anguished amazement, Feyzi saw Safiyeh, as white and fleeting as an unattainable dream. He saw her arched eyebrows, proud and commanding, and he felt himself surrender. As though he was waging battle with unbridled powers, unarmed but fearlessly combating invisible forces. Standing at the window, the threshold of a newly emerging world, he wanted to embrace the future in his sturdy arms. And he was unaware that it had already gripped him with its talons as it devoured him with a violent, insatiable appetite.

Bibliography - Մատենագիտություն

"Yashmakë – Arevelki Gyankén" ["The Yashmak: On Life in the Orient"], *Anahid* (Constantinople), Ed. Arshag/Archag Chobanian, Nov. – Dec. 1899, pp. 11 – 13.

«Եաշմակը – Արեւելքի Կեանքէն», Անահիտ (Պոլիս), Խմբ. Արշակ Չօպանեան, Նոյ. – Դեկտ. 1899, էջ 11 – 13:

"Ir Adelutyunë" ["His Hate"], *Daretsuyts* (Constantinople), Ed. Nshan Babigian, Year II, 1906, pp. 166 – 172.

«Իր Ատելութիւնը», Տարեցոյց (Պոլիս), Խմբ. Նշան Պապիկեան, Բ. Տարի, 1906, էջ 166 – 172:

"Anedzkë" ["The Curse"], *Azadamard Daily* (Constantinople), Ed. Rupen Zartarian, June 26 – Jul. 1, 1911.

«Անէծքը», Ազատամարտ օրաթերթ (Պոլիս), Խմբ. Ռուբէն Զարդարեան, Յունիս 26 – Յուլ. 1, 1911:

"Safiyeh," *Azadamard Weekly – Supplement* (Constantinople), Ed. Rupen Zartarian, No. 13 (65), 9/22 October 1911, pp. 4 (1028) – 9 (1033).

«Սաֆիէ», Ազատամարտ Շաբաթաթերթ – Յաւելուած (Պոլիս), Խմբ. Ռուբէն Զարդարեան, Թիւ 13 (65), 9/22 Հոկտեմբեր 1911, էջ 4 (1028) – 9 (1033):

"Nor Harsë" ["The New Bride"], *Azadamard Weekly – Supplement* (Constantinople), Ed. Rupen Zartarian, No. 39, March 10/April 23, 1911, pp. 3 (601) – 5 (603).

«Նոր Հարսը», Ազատամարտ Շաբաթաթերթ – Յաւելուած (Պոլիս), Խմբ. Ռուբէն Զարդարեան, Թիւ 39, Մարտ 10/Ապրիլ 23, 1911, էջ 3 (601) – 5 (603):

"Parkë" ["The Glory"], *Hay Kraganutyun* (Izmir), Ed. Zareh Kazazian, No. 6, 1/14 Feb. 1913, pp. 13 – 17.

«Փառք», Հայ Գրականութիւն (Զմիւռնեա), Խմբ. Զարեհ Գազազեան, Թիւ 6, 1/14 Փետր., 1913, էջ 13 – 17:

"Sbasumë" ["The Wait"], *Azadamard Daily* (Constantinople), Ed. Rupen Zartarian, Jan. 1 – 14, 1914, p. 3.

«Սպասումը», Ազատամարտ օրաթերթ (Պոլիս), Խմբ. Ռուբէն Զարդարեան, Յունուար 1 – 14, 1914, էջ 3:

"Turk Gnoch Azadakrutyan Hartsë" ["On the Question of Turkish Women's Emancipation"], *Azadamard Daily* (Constantinople), Ed. Rupen Zartarian, Jan. 18/13, 1914, No. 1418, p. 1.

«Թուրք Կնոջ Ազատագրութեան Հարցը», Ազատամարտ օրաթերթ (Պոլիս), Խմբ. Ռուբէն Զարդարեան, Յունուար 18/31, 1914, Թիւ 1418, էջ 1:

"Turk Gnoch Gyanken – Namehramë" ["The Namehram: Life as a Turkish Woman"], *Azadamard Daily* (Constantinople), Ed. Rupen Zartarian, Jan. 26 – Feb. 3, 1914, No. 1425, p. 1.

«Թուրք Կնոջ Կեանքէն – Նամէհրամը», Ազատամարտ օրաթերթ (Պոլիս), Խմբ. Ռուբէն Զարդարեան, Յունուար 26 – Փետր. 3, 1914, Թիւ 1425, էջ 1:

Yerp Aylevs Chen Sirer; Koghë; Vebë [*When They Love No More; The Veil; The Novel*], (Constantinople), Haig Goshgarian Publishing, Printed by O. Arzuman, 1914.[*]

Երբ Այլեւս Չեն Սիրեր; Քողը; Վէպը, (Պոլիս), Հայկ Կոշկարեան Գրատուն, Տպարան եւ կազմատուն O. Արզուման, 1914:

"Mangan më Mahë" ["The Death of a Child"], *Piunig* (Boston), No. 2, March 1919, pp. 903 – 907.

«Մանկան մը Մահը», Փիւնիկ (Պոստոն), Թիւ 2, Մարտ 1919, էջ 903 – 907:

"Semin Vra – Badgerner Trkagan Gyanké" ["On the Threshold: Scenes from Life in Turkey"], *Arek* (Berlin), No. 18, Dec. 1924, pp. 1089 – 1106.

«Սեմին Վրայ – Պատկերներ Թրքական Կեանքէ» Արեգ (Պերլին), Թիւ 18, Դեկտ. 1924, էջ 1089 – 1106:

Meliha Nuri Hanëm (Veb), (Paris), Daron Publishing, 1928.[*]
Մելիհա Նուրի Հանըմ (Վեպ), *(Փարիզ), Տպարան «Տարոն», 1928:*

The Veil and *Meliha Nuri Hanum* were translated into English by G. M. Goshgarian and published in the collection, *Captive Nights: From the Bosphorus to Gallipoli with Zabel Yessayan*, Ed. Nanor Kebranian (The Press at California State University, 2021).

Biographical Note: Nanor Kebranian is a researcher, writer, and translator working at the intersection of history, literature, and law. She received her doctorate from Oxford University with fellowships from the Jack Kent Cooke Foundation and Oxford's Clarendon Fund. In addition to her appointment as Assistant Professor in the Department of Middle Eastern, South Asian, and African Studies at Columbia University, she has also held research positions at Queen Mary University of London and Nanyang Technological University, Singapore. She has commissioned and edited several published translations of Armenian literature and scholarship, as well as publishing her own translations of poetry by Krikor Beledian and Tanyel Varoujan.

www.ingramcontent.com/pod-product-compliance
Lightning Source LLC
Chambersburg PA
CBHW030036030726
47500CB00001B/129